Megan Parnell Mysteries

Trouble in Yakima Valley

For my dear son and daughter-in-love,
Rob and Lydia Biggar

MYSTERIES
MEGAN PARNELL
MP

Trouble in Yakima Valley

Joan Rawlins Biggar

CPH
SAINT LOUIS

Megan Parnell Mysteries

Missing on Castaway Island
Mystery at Camp Galena
Trouble in Yakima Valley

Cover illustration by Matthew Archambault.

Scripture quotations taken from the HOLY BIBLE, NEW INTERNATIONAL VERSION®. NIV®. Copyright © 1973, 1978, 1984 by International Bible Society. Used by permission of Zondervan Publishing House. All rights reserved.

Copyright © 1998 Concordia Publishing House
3558 South Jefferson Avenue
St. Louis, MO 63118-3968
Manufactured in the United States of America

Library of Congress Cataloging-in-Publication Data
Biggar, Joan Rawlins, 1936-
    Trouble in Yakima Valley / Joan Rawlins Biggar.
        p.   cm. — (Megan Parnell mysteries ; 3)
    Summary: Sixteen-year-olds Megan and Peter expose the bullies who are sabotaging their uncle's apple harvest and persecuting an Hispanic family working in the orchards of Yakima, Washington.
    ISBN 0-570-05031-6
    [1. Orchards—Fiction. 2. Christian life—Fiction. 3. Washington (State)—Fiction. 4. Mystery and detective stories.] I. Title.
II. Series: Biggar, Joan Rawlins, 1936- Megan Parnell mysteries:
3.
PZ7.B483Tt   1998   97-18134
[Fic]—DC21   AC

1 2 3 4 5 6 7 8 9 10   07 06 05 04 03 02 01 00 99 98

Contents

A Whole New
Way of Life

Megan Parnell sucked in a breath of air so frosty it almost hurt. She pushed back her thick brown hair, then squatted next to her stepbrother, Peter Lewis, to splash icy Yakima River water over her face.

Peter's dog, Jiggs, poked a speckled muzzle over her shoulder. He nudged her cheek with a nose even icier than the water.

"Cut it out, Jiggs!" After an uncomfortable, colder-than-expected night in the tent, Megan was in no mood for a romp. She stood up stiffly, wiping drips from her chin with fingers that tingled, and zipped her jacket all the way up.

The dog, a mostly black mix of spaniel and Labrador retriever, cocked his head at her with a puzzled expression. He turned to Peter, begging him to play. Peter was splashing sleep from his eyes and didn't respond. Jiggs gave up and waded into the river to lap a drink.

April sunshine scattered a million diamonds across the chortling water. As Megan watched them sparkle, her bad mood began to evaporate. Spending Easter weekend in Yakima with an elderly couple she didn't even know hadn't been her idea of a good time. In spite of herself, she'd liked the Wirths when she met them yesterday. But camping—that could wait until summer.

Peter jumped to his feet. Droplets flew as he shook his auburn head. "Brrr! Did you stay warm last night?"

"No!"

"Me either. Those winter-rated sleeping bags must be meant for southern California, not eastern Washington!"

Jiggs bounded out of the water, stopped between them, and shook himself. They both yelled and tried to dodge the cold shower.

School in Madrona Bay had let out early yesterday for the Easter weekend. Megan and Peter, both 16 and sophomores, had piled into the minivan with their parents and crossed the Cascade Mountains to Yakima, arriving in time for supper with Peter's great-uncle Martin Wirth and his wife, Gladys. Uncle Martin had let slip in a phone conversation that things on the apple ranch weren't going well. Darren Lewis, Megan's stepfather of less than a year, hoped their visit would offer encouragement.

Although the Wirths had invited them to sleep at the ranch last night, they'd gone ahead with their planned camp-out. Megan glanced across the campground at the tents. Her mother, Sarah, broke eggs into a bowl at the picnic table while Darren hovered over a panful of frying bacon at the fire. A breeze brought a whiff of the mouth-watering scent.

Jiggs raised his head and stared downriver. Megan turned to see a small boy ambling around the bend, tossing stones into the water. His skinny brown arms and legs stuck out of a too-big T-shirt and short pants.

His face lit with a grin as he spied a stick floating past. He splashed into the river after it. "He can't be more than 4 years old," Megan muttered, scanning the shore. Wasn't anyone watching him?

The boy reached for the stick and slipped. His tousled black head disappeared under the water. In a moment it popped up, streaming wet. "¡Caramba!" she heard him exclaim. His arms thrashed the water, then he went under again.

Megan's feet felt rooted in cement. She heard a scream and realized it was her own.

Peter shouted, "I'm coming!" He dashed past her and into the river. Jiggs began to bark. She found her wits and scrambled after Peter.

The river was barely over Peter's knees, but too deep and swift for such a small boy to regain his footing. Peter grabbed him around the chest and carried him, choking and coughing, to shore. Megan reached to help.

Suddenly a slender whirlwind with tumbling black hair pushed between them. She caught the child in her arms. "Teodoro! Oh, Teodoro!" She dropped to her knees, hugging and patting him. "Naughty Teodoro! What will mamacita say?"

Megan glimpsed a couple of wide-eyed little girls running toward the group on the riverbank. Mom and Darren hurried toward them from the other direction.

"My boat ..." Teodoro struggled to free himself from the girl's embrace, pointing toward the river. "He sail away." Then he stopped struggling and laughed with

9

delight. Jiggs had gone after the stick. He swam back to shore, shook himself, and dropped it at Teodoro's feet.

The girl lifted dark eyes, misty with gratitude, to Peter's. "I was helping the little ones wash, and he slipped away ... thank you! Oh, thank you for saving him!"

Sarah and Darren arrived. "Everything all right?" asked Peter's dad.

The girl stood up, holding fast to her little brother's hand, and nodded. Her hair was glossy and thick and fell in ripples halfway to her waist. Though obviously shaken, she managed a smile. "Teodoro's not afraid of anything. I cannot take my eyes away for a minute."

She turned to the younger girls. "Alicia, Isabel, take him to mamacita." She spoke with a charming accent. Megan noted the bemused expression on Peter's face. Obviously, he found more than her accent charming. The girls took their brother's hands and hurried away.

"That was quick thinking, Peter!" Darren commented.

"Peter?" The girl held out her hand. "I am Rosalía Salinas. My mamá and papá and all my brothers and sisters thank you too."

Peter blushed self-consciously. "It was nothing," he said. He glanced sideways at Megan. "The water wasn't very deep."

"Maybe so," Megan said. "But you didn't know that. And I was too scared to even move." She turned to Rosalía. "I'm Megan Parnell," she said. "These are our parents." The grown-ups smiled hello, then turned back to the campsite.

10

"Do you live near here?" Peter asked.

"We are camping over there," Rosalía answered, gesturing toward a clump of willows some distance back from the river.

Peter glanced down at the wet pant legs sticking to his calves, then watched the children disappear around the bend. "It's cold this morning," he said. "How can they stand running around without jackets?"

Long lashes fanned against her cheeks as Rosalía looked down at her frayed canvas shoes. "It will soon be warm." She pulled her thin sweater tighter around her. "I must find dry clothes for Teodoro. Thank you again. Good-bye!"

"Good-bye." Megan and Peter watched her run along the beach and around the bend.

"How can any of those children be warm enough?" Peter shivered. Megan heard water squishing in his shoes as they hurried back to their own campsite.

"Get into dry clothes," Sarah called. "Some hot breakfast will help warm you up."

Peter disappeared into his pup tent to change. When he joined them at the picnic table, Darren held out his hands. "Let's sing our blessing this morning," he said. They all joined hands while their voices rose in the crisp morning air.

> Praise God, from whom all blessings flow;
> Praise Him, all creatures here below;
> Praise Him above, O heav'nly host;
> Praise Father, Son, and Holy Ghost.

"And Heavenly Father," Darren added, "thank You that Peter and Megan were in the right place this morning to rescue that little boy. Bless him and his family. And please help us always to be ready to do Your work."

"Amen," added the others.

Megan's mom passed the platter of scrambled eggs and bacon. "The sun is so pleasant this morning," she said. "I can't believe how cold we got last night. I'd just as soon stay at Uncle Martin's house tonight."

"I wondered if you outdoors types weren't starting the camping season a little early," Darren commented. "When I was a boy, I often visited the Wirths during spring vacation. It usually got pretty cold at night. Once or twice I helped them fight frost in the orchards. Remember, Peter, I told you about that?"

"Yeah," Peter said. "Once, you said, it even snowed after the apple trees were in bloom."

"Well," Darren said to his wife, "with the kids' visit to the packing plant today and such a short time to spend with Martin and Gladys, I think you're right. Let's forget camping until later in the season."

When they finished eating, Megan piled the dishes into a dishpan full of soapy water. Peter helped his father roll up the sleeping bags and take down the tents. Then he walked over to where Megan was packing the clean dishes into their basket. "I'd like to check on Teodoro," he told her. "Want to come along?"

"You're sure it's Teodoro you want to check on?" Megan gave him a mischievous look and grinned. "Sure, I'll go. We'll be right back," she called to her mom.

Megan and Peter followed the riverbank to the bend, then headed toward the yellow-green willows. Jiggs trotted ahead.

12

"Pretty fancy camping," Megan commented, waving her hand as they passed a couple of luxury coaches sprouting TV antennae, awnings, and air-conditioners.

"Somehow I don't think Rosalía's family will be camping in one of those," Peter replied.

"No, I'm sure they won't. Look." Megan nodded toward the grove of willows.

A big, dented van with faded paint sat half-hidden in the trees with a two-wheeled trailer behind it. The van's open sliding door revealed rumpled bedding on the floor and seats. A clear plastic sheet over the trailer revealed mattresses, chairs, and other household belongings.

Isabel and Alicia, with Teodoro between them, sat at a picnic table where pots and dishes and a box of food were piled.

A weary-looking woman lifted a kettle from the fire and brought it to the table. "Come, Rosalía," she called, ladling a spoonful of beans onto a tortilla and rolling it up.

"Coming, mamacita." Rosalía appeared in the doorway of the van, carrying a plump toddler on her hip. She saw Peter and Megan and her face lit up. Quickly, she stepped down. Shifting the child to the other hip, she slid the door shut.

She spoke to her mother in Spanish.

The woman handed the tortilla to Teodoro and turned to the visitors, her tired face brightening in a smile.

"This is my mother, Magdalena Salinas," Rosalía said. "Mamá, this is Peter and Megan."

13

Jiggs, his tail wagging, watched the tortilla. "Sit, Jiggs," Peter said. "Buenos días, Mrs. Salinas."

Mrs. Salinas erupted into a flood of Spanish, smiling and shaking their hands.

"Now what do I do?" Peter whispered to Megan. "Those were the only two Spanish words I know."

"My mamá says you saved her little boy's life," Rosalía translated. "She says she thanks you—anything we have is yours. She says will you sit down and have some breakfast?"

Mrs. Salinas nodded and smiled.

"Mamá understands English pretty well," said Rosalía. "But it's hard for her to speak it."

Megan turned to Mrs. Salinas. "Thank you. We just ate breakfast."

"How is Teodoro?" Peter asked.

The little boy, dressed in another too-big T-shirt, ducked his head and grinned with his mouth full of tortilla.

"Teodoro good," his mother beamed. "He okay." She quickly rolled tortillas for Rosalía's younger sisters, then reached for the plump baby. "This one Juan."

"You're lucky to have so many brothers and sisters, Rosalía," Peter told her. "I didn't have anybody until my dad and Megan's mom got married."

"I have another brother," Rosalía said. "Luis. We are both 16."

"Twins!" Megan exclaimed. "I always thought it would be fun to have a twin. Peter and I are 16 too, but I'm a few months older."

"Where is Luis?" Peter asked.

14

"He went with papá to see if they could find work for us."

Megan's eyes widened. "You kids work too? What about school?"

"We go to school. Sometimes regular school. Sometimes Luis and I go at night."

Isabel slid off the bench and patted Jiggs. "I'm in third grade," she said with pride.

Peter glanced around the campsite. "Is ... is this where you live all the time?"

"Oh, no," Rosalía said, looking embarrassed. "Just since the man we worked for went out of business. When we find work, we will move into a house again."

"A big house," Isabel said. "And we will get a nice dog, like yours."

Mrs. Salinas smiled and hugged the little girl. "Isabel dream big," she said.

Megan tried to think of something to say. "Big dreams are the best kind," she answered. "We'd better go now, Peter. Our folks will be ready to leave."

She and Peter said good-bye. They walked for a while in silence toward their own campsite.

"Rosalía and her family are homeless, aren't they?" Peter's clear blue eyes clouded with thought.

"Maybe," Megan answered, uncertain. "Maybe they're migrant workers. Maybe that's just the way they live."

"That could be," he said. "Uncle Martin says growers here couldn't get along without migrant labor. It's a whole different way of life, isn't it?"

15

Apples from Start to Finish

With their camping equipment piled in the back of the minivan, the Lewis family rolled west through the streets of Yakima. They passed a fancy motor home like those they'd seen in the campground. Megan compared it and her own comfortable home with the battered van that was both home and transportation for the Salinas family. It just didn't seem fair that some people had so much and others so little.

Peter interrupted her thoughts. "Look," he exclaimed, pointing to a sign. "The advertising on some of the businesses is in Spanish as well as English."

Darren turned up the radio. A young woman's voice, speaking Spanish, filled the car. Lively music followed. "Some of the radio and TV stations here use only Spanish," he said over his shoulder. "I like the music even if I don't understand the words."

Near the outskirts of town where the buildings thinned, Megan gazed across the wide valley. Orchards patterned hazy hills in the distance. On this side of the valley, the road wound past orchards of trees misted with tiny new leaves and clusters of pink buds just beginning to open.

"Uncle Martin said the bee man was coming this morning," Peter remarked.

"The *what* man?" Megan exclaimed.

"Didn't you see the bee hives in the orchards we passed? Uncle Martin says the person who owns the bees takes them from orchard to orchard so they can pollinate the blooms."

"Just so they stay away from me," she said.

"Don't worry," he teased. "You're not sweet enough for them to bother you."

Megan grimaced at him.

Darren turned the minivan onto a side road that twisted farther up into the hills. After a while, he slowed and turned again onto a gravel road. Megan saw an old house settled comfortably against the curve of a hill.

"Isn't that where Uncle Martin and Aunt Gladys lived when you were growing up?" Peter asked his father.

Darren nodded. "After they moved, they rented the old place to their foreman. It's empty now. Uncle Martin told me his last foreman just left. Some large orchardist promised him more money."

"Gladys told me that same company is pressuring them to sell their orchards," Sarah said quietly. "Martin refused."

"Why is their property so important to a big company?" Megan wanted to know.

"I asked her that," Sarah said. "She doesn't know for sure. Maybe it's because the company already owns most of the orchards surrounding them. And the Wirths do have a good well—a valuable source of irrigation water—right there on the ranch."

18

The gravel road continued to climb until it ended in front of a neat, split-level house. Apple trees grew up to the lawn at one side and continued up the hill in back.

A small woman with short white hair hurried out of the house and down the steps to meet them. Brown eyes twinkled behind her glasses.

"Here we are again, Aunt Gladys," called Peter's dad. "It took a while for the sunshine to thaw our cold bones this morning. We all agreed we'd like to stay with you tonight."

"You know we'd love to have you." Gladys Wirth's face crinkled into a maze of smile lines. "Martin and I worried about you last night."

Peter opened the door of the van. Jiggs leaped out, dragging his master behind on his leash. Megan followed more slowly, still feeling somewhat shy.

"Come in, everybody, the coffeepot's on. Martin's out in the orchard. But he's all set to take Peter and Megan to the packing plant."

The Wirths' son-in-law, Kevin Kronheim, whom they'd also met last night, worked at a nearby apple packing plant and had offered to show them around.

"Has the bee man been here yet, Aunt Gladys?" Peter asked.

"Yes, and gone again. Do you want to find Uncle Martin and tell him you're here?"

"Sure." Peter unsnapped the leash so Jiggs could run free. "Come on, Megan."

They walked along the tractor road Aunt Gladys pointed out, peering down rows of blooming trees until they caught a glimpse of Martin Wirth's cap and plaid shirt. Jiggs trotted ahead, tail wagging, to investigate.

Megan flinched as a bee zoomed past her ear. Uncle Martin saw her duck and chuckled. "They're already at work. We set the hives over here, along the fence line." He led them between the trees to the edge of the orchard where a wire fence separated the cultivated land from the bunchgrass covered hills.

The hives were a row of white painted boxes stacked along the fence. Megan hung back, not wanting to get too close. As they watched, a few bees crawled out of the opening in the front of the nearest box, turned this way and that, orienting themselves, then zipped away.

"You've heard the term *making a beeline*?" Uncle Martin asked Megan. "Watch. You'll see them fly along the edge of the orchard until they reach the row where the tree they're working on is located. Back and forth, always the fastest route."

"Like a bee superhighway," she commented. She gave a little squeal as another bee zoomed past her head.

"Just stay calm and don't move too fast," the old man said with a smile. "They won't bother you."

"These trees have more flowers open than some we passed," Peter noted.

"That's because it's a little warmer up here on the hill. Different kinds of apples blossom at different times too. When the bees have finished these trees, other orchards will be ready for pollination."

"If even a small part of these blossoms turn into apples, you should have a wonderful crop," Megan commented.

"Yes, Lord willing." Martin Wirth turned his leathery face up to the masses of pink and white above them. "But many things have to go just right from the time the trees blossom to when the fruit gets to market. We walk a narrow line between success and disaster in this business, but there's nothing I'd rather do than grow my apples."

Megan thought of her mother's earlier remark. Obviously the Wirths loved their life on the apple ranch. It would be horrible if some big, impersonal company forced them to give it up.

They returned through the fragrant orchard to the ranch buildings. Uncle Martin took time for a cup of coffee with their parents. While they talked, he mentioned that he'd surprised a couple of trespassers in the orchard early that morning. "They'd parked around the curve in the road where we couldn't see them from the house. Long-haired, scraggly looking characters with old army surplus backpacks and muddy boots. One had a pick-ax. Said they were rock hunters coming down from the ridge back there. Could have been rock hounds ... they sure looked like they'd been digging."

"What did you do?" asked Darren.

"Told them about some of the places local rock hounds like to go. They said thanks anyway and high-tailed it down the drive. I heard them start their engine and drive away."

He set down his coffee cup. "Ready, you two?" He led Megan and Peter outside to his crew-cab pickup.

"Will we see some of your apples at the packing plant?" Megan asked him.

21

"Ours, and apples from lots of other orchards too," he answered, starting the engine. "Last fall all the ranchers sent their apples to the packing plant where they were put into cold storage. Workers sort and pack them and ship them all over the country, as the market demands."

They drove past orchard after orchard until they came to a small community. Big, windowless buildings loomed behind the homes along the main street.

"Peter's been here before, so he knows those are the cold storage buildings," Uncle Martin said, turning up a side street and then into a paved yard in front of a complex of buildings. A sign above a glassed-in office said *Western Packers*.

"Kevin's around someplace." He parked beside some other vehicles. "He's the outside boss here."

A truck growled past them and backed into a loading bay next to the building. "There he is," said Peter. A tall man dressed in jeans and a denim jacket waved from a cluster of people in front of the office.

"Job seekers," Kevin said as he approached. "They're filling out applications, though we've got all the crew we need right now." He held out a big, callused hand to Megan. "Hi, Peter's new sister." Pale eyebrows and white teeth contrasted sharply with his tanned face. "Welcome. Glad you both took me up on the invitation to see what we do here."

"Thank you. It sounds interesting," said Megan.

"Come on then. Our floor lady will give you the royal tour."

They followed him past the job applicants sitting outside the office, filling out papers. Most of the people were Hispanic, Megan noticed. One, a boy about their age, helped an older man with his paper.

Inside, they had to shout to be heard above the noise of machinery. Kevin introduced them to Madge, the floor supervisor, then he and Uncle Martin went back outside.

The first thing Megan noticed were the conveyor belts at differing heights, moving the fruit through the long building. Apples rolled from the belts down chutes onto revolving tables where workers put them into plastic bags.

Madge beckoned them to follow her past the rumbling machinery into another big room where four-foot-square boxes of apples sat stacked against the wall.

"Those bins have been in controlled atmosphere storage," she said. "When they come in from the orchards, they are stacked 12 high in storage rooms. Most of the oxygen is pumped out of the rooms, and the temperature is set just above freezing. The apples keep for a year that way.

"When we get an order for apples, the bins are brought here. When the apples reach the temperature of this room, we process them." She indicated a man wheeling a forklift over to the bins. "Watch."

The man maneuvered the tines of the fork under one of the bins, lifted it, and drove toward them. Madge led them up some metal steps overlooking a deep tank of water. The forklift operator hoisted the bin, then lowered it into the tank. The apples bobbed to the surface.

The moving water floated them onto a conveyor that carried them into the sorting building.

They followed Madge back through the door to a platform overlooking the area where the conveyor entered the building. A row of women, their hands a blur of motion, sorted apples onto three conveyor belts, one above the other. The women looked up and smiled. Megan noticed that none of them were Hispanic and wondered why. "The water washed away the dust and dirt," Madge said. "Now we grade them for size and quality."

"Why are they all greenish?" Megan asked. "Aren't they ripe?"

"Yes, they're ripe. They're Golden Delicious," Madge answered. "We grow a lot of Red Delicious around here too."

They followed her down a catwalk alongside rolling metal rods that moved the apples to a machine that sprayed them with a thin protective coating of wax. Spinning brushes polished them shiny. Then they dropped onto conveyors which sorted them into boxes or rolled them out onto the revolving tables Megan had noticed earlier.

"If they're not perfect, they're sent elsewhere to be made into juice or sauce or maybe pie filling," Madge said. They watched the workers at the revolving tables fill five-pound plastic bags with small apples and pack them into cardboard boxes. "You've probably seen these at the grocery store."

"Would you like a sample?" one of the workers asked. She handed a just-filled bag to Peter.

Beyond her work station, a machine folded and glued the cardboard box tops, then bound the boxes with plastic bands.

"This is the last step," Madge told them as the conveyor carried the boxes into another room, where a man stacked them. "From here they go to the customers."

Megan and Peter thanked Madge for the tour and stepped out of the cool building into the sunshine.

"After all that, I'll never take my lunchtime apple for granted again," Megan exclaimed.

"Me either," said Peter. "Want to try one of our samples?" He offered her a greenish globe. She bit into it. Juicy and snapping crisp, it tasted as good as it smelled.

"There's Uncle Martin." Peter pointed past the parked vehicles to where his uncle and Kevin were examining a strange-looking truck. It had an ordinary cab, but it pulled a tall, open structure of metal beams.

Megan followed as Peter started toward the two men. The group of people by the office had broken up. One of them, a burly, red-faced man who'd stood apart from the others while filling out his papers, strode to his car and got in. The older Hispanic man and the teenager walked over to him.

Megan didn't hear the question, but she and Peter both heard the answer, loud and clear. "Don't ask me for a ride. You beaners take over our town, take the jobs, then you have the gall to expect us to drive you where you want to go." The red-faced man banged his door shut. Gravel spurted from his tires as he gunned his car onto the street.

The teenager's handsome, high cheek-boned face flushed dark. The older man shrugged. They started on foot down the driveway.

Megan and Peter walked over to Kevin and Uncle Martin, who apparently hadn't noticed the unpleasant little scene. "Well, Megan," Uncle Martin said as they came up, "this morning in the orchard you saw the beginning of the industry cycle. Now you've seen the end, except for getting the apples to the stores and out to your kitchen. What did you think?"

"Very interesting," Megan answered. "I'd like to see what happens when the orchards are ready for harvest."

"Then consider yourself invited to come back in the fall."

Megan inspected the funny-looking truck. Inside the outer framework, two rails were suspended, parallel to and close to the ground. "What is this thing?" she asked.

"It's a straddle buggy," said Kevin. "During harvest, they run between orchards and packing plants carrying the bins of apples like you saw inside."

"They carry up to eight bins, end to end, stacked four bins high," commented Uncle Martin.

Peter whistled. "That's a lot of apples!"

"Sure is," agreed his uncle. "Well, Kevin, thanks. See you at the Easter sunrise service tomorrow?"

"Sure thing."

Megan and Peter thanked him too and said good-bye. As Uncle Martin headed the pickup through the little town, they rolled down the windows to cool the sun-heated crew-cab. Ahead, two people thrust out their thumbs in a hitchhiker's plea.

Uncle Martin slowed. "Those two were filling out applications at Western Packers, weren't they?"

"Yes. They asked one of the other guys for a ride," said Peter.

"He was really nasty to them," added Megan.

Uncle Martin stopped the pickup and backed up while the teenager and the older man jogged toward them. "Gracias, señor." The two scrambled into the bed of the pickup.

Uncle Martin leaned out the window. "Where are you heading?"

"Yakima," answered the boy. "Or far as you are going."

As they rode along, Peter turned to look at the hitch-hikers. They sat with their backs to the window, hair blowing in the wind. "Rosalía said her father and brother were looking for work today."

Uncle Martin looked at him inquiringly. Peter told him the story of little Teodoro and the family in the campground.

"It's sad that people must live like that," Martin Wirth replied.

When they reached the road to the ranch, they stopped to let the two in back climb out.

"Muchas gracias," the man said. Then he spoke to the boy in Spanish.

The boy glanced at Megan and Peter, then away. He turned to Uncle Martin. "My father thanks you," he

27

translated. He hesitated, as if the next words stuck in his throat. "He asks if you need any work done."

"I'll be hiring a few people when the fruit sets on, to do the thinning," said Uncle Martin. "Check back." He told them his name. "What are your names?"

"My father is Carlos," said the boy. "Carlos Salinas. My name is Luis."

Bees and Freeze

t *is* them!" exclaimed Megan.

"Luis Salinas?" Peter leaned out the window. "Do you have a sister named Rosalia?"

Surprise flickered in the boy's face. How do you know about my sister?"

Peter told how they'd met Teodoro and the rest of the family at the campground that morning.

Mr. Salinas listened closely. Evidently, like his wife, he understood English better than he spoke it. "Ah, Teodoro!" He shook his head. "Such a one!" He reached to shake Peter's hand. "Gracias, amigo."

Mr. Salinas and Luis trudged away as Uncle Martin turned the pickup toward the ranch. Megan watched until a bend in the road hid them from view. Rosalía had said Luis and his dad were looking for work for all of them. Kids their age should be in school, not working to support their family. She wished she knew some way to help.

Later, after homemade soup and some of Aunt Gladys' apple pie, Megan and Peter wandered outside. Darren Lewis and Uncle Martin were loading some strange-looking objects into the back of the pickup.

"These are smudge pots," Peter's dad told Megan. "Oil goes in the container here, at the bottom." He picked up a metal canister with a long tube jutting from the top. "We light them with this torch. Heat radiates from the tall chimneys and keeps the blossoms from freezing."

"Where are you taking them?" Megan asked.

"To the Wirths' other orchard further down the valley. Usually they're left in the orchard year round. These needed repair."

"I didn't see any smudge pots here." Megan indicated the nearby trees.

"We have our own well and irrigation pond near this orchard, so we ice these trees. See those pipes sticking above the trees? Those are the sprinklers," Uncle Martin said. "Some people use wind machines." Megan had noticed the much taller wind machines in other orchards. Their big propellers pulled warm air down to tree level.

The men lifted the last smudge pot into the truck. She wondered how using ice could keep the trees from freezing, but before she could ask, Uncle Martin slid behind the wheel and started the engine. "We won't be gone long," he called.

"Is it okay if we explore up there?" Peter called back, indicating the slopes above the orchard.

"Fine."

"Aunt Gladys said we could dye eggs," Megan said to Peter. "Tomorrow's Easter, you know."

"That's kid stuff."

"C'mon. It's tradition."

"Maybe later. Let's go see what's up on the hill." Peter whistled for Jiggs. The three walked across the

30

lawn behind the house and up a lane between blossom-laden branches.

"Listen," she said. They stopped. The perfumed air throbbed with a faint humming.

"It's the bees," Peter said.

She watched a bee dip into a cluster of blooms, pushing and probing for nectar. Yellow pollen clung to the hairs on its body. The bee combed itself with its legs, packing the pollen into "baskets" that were part of its back legs.

At the edge of the orchard, Peter held strands of barbed wire apart while Megan climbed through. Jiggs zigzagged up the hill ahead of them, following interesting smells. Suddenly he yipped and began to dig frantically. Dirt flew as he tried to follow the retreat of some animal deep into its burrow.

"Probably a rockchuck," Peter said. "They're marmots, something like woodchucks." He couldn't distract Jiggs, so they left him digging.

"It's hot!" Megan exclaimed, taking off her jacket and tying it around her waist. Finally they reached a jumble of rocks near the crest of the hill. Peter checked for sunning rattlesnakes, then plopped down on a rock. Megan found herself a comfortable spot and leaned back to enjoy the view. Bird songs spiraled through the air. Below, the Wirths' home looked like a toy house snuggled into a corduroy quilt of apple trees. Clumps of yellow balsamroot sunflowers splashed the green hill around them.

"I'm glad we're here now," Peter said. "In summer, all this green will turn tan and prickly. Not the orchards though," he said. "Water makes the difference."

"Uncle Martin said more fruit grows in the Yakima Valley than anyplace else in the United States."

"Yes, thanks to irrigation." Peter laughed and pointed down the hill. "Look at Jiggs." The dog crouched on his forelegs, nose in the rockchuck burrow, his rear pointing skyward. "Come on. Let's see if he's found his quarry."

By the time they reached Jiggs, he'd given up. He lay panting by the hole, his floppy ears and muzzle dusted with dirt, but when he saw them he leaped up, ready to go.

They wandered down the hill, angling away from the ravine to the far side of the orchard. They followed the fence until they neared the hives.

"Let's go a little farther before we crawl through the fence," Peter said. "Those bees are working their little tails off. I don't want to get in their way."

"Lead on."

They passed the hives. Megan stopped suddenly. "Look, Peter!" Cautiously, she moved toward the fence. An egg-shaped mass hung from a branch on the other side. "It's bees!" she cried, stepping back. "Hundreds and hundreds of bees!"

A few insects flew around the black, quivering mass, then settled down to become part of it.

"They must be swarming," said Peter.

"They must be what?"

"Getting ready to look for another nest. We'd better tell Uncle Martin."

"I hope he's back."

They climbed through the wire fence, then raced through the orchard. They found the rancher in the backyard and quickly told him about the swarm.

Peter told Jiggs to stay. The three of them started back through the orchard. "The beekeeper told me he thought one hive was getting pretty full," Uncle Martin said. "He left an extra, just in case."

The mass of bees still hung from the branch.

"Isn't it dangerous to try to capture them?" Megan asked.

"They fill up with honey before they swarm, so they're not very alert. All they want is to stay with their queen." Uncle Martin got the empty hive and set it down next to the tree. He took some twine from his pocket and tied his pant legs around his ankles. "I got stung once when I forgot to tie my pants. I didn't know some had crawled up inside until I knelt down."

He picked up a stick. "What we do," he said, "is hit the branch and knock them to the ground. I head the queen toward the hive and the others will follow."

"You're kidding!" Megan exclaimed. "There are thousands of bees! How can you possibly find the queen?"

"She'll be much bigger than the others."

"Let me hit the branch," Peter said.

Uncle Martin handed him the stick. "One quick rap, then step back so I can find her Royal Highness."

"Be careful, Peter."

He sent a confident grin her way. "Nothing to it. Watch this!" He aimed the stick at a spot next to the swarm, swung, and connected.

He stepped backwards, caught his foot in weeds, and crashed into Megan. She slammed onto her back, the breath knocked out of her. Overhead, the swarm of bees poured from the branch like a living waterfall, spilling onto Megan's legs, flowing slowly over her prostrate body.

Megan found her breath and shrieked. A strong hand gripped her shoulder and held her to the ground. Uncle Martin spoke quietly in her ear, "Don't move."

He reached into the mass of bees crawling toward her head. "Here she is," he said, nudging the queen gently across Megan's chest, over her right shoulder. He signaled Peter to bring the hive closer. "Easy, Megan."

The army of insects neared her head. Her heart thumped so wildly she felt sure it must be bouncing the humming creatures up and down. Desperately she prayed, *Lord, please don't let them get mad.*

"Lie perfectly still," Uncle Martin whispered.

Megan clenched her lips tight to keep from shrieking again as some of the insects crawled up her bare throat, over her chin and cheeks and tightly shut eyelids. Their marching feet prickled. Some of them got caught in her hair and buzzed.

After an eternity, Uncle Martin said, "You're okay now."

Megan opened her eyes and slowly turned her head. The last of the swarm flowed like a waterfall in reverse through the opening at the bottom of the hive.

She glared into her stepbrother's worried eyes. "Good going, Peter!"

"Sorry." With a sheepish smile, he helped her up. She untied the jacket around her waist and shook it. One or two bees dropped from its folds. "I ought to put those down your neck," she told him and stalked away.

Peter hurried to catch up. "Don't be mad, Megan," he pleaded. "I'll help you dye Easter eggs."

Megan allowed herself a small grin. "All right. I'll hold you to it."

～～～～～～

Delicious smells filled the kitchen.

At the stove, Aunt Gladys stirred a pot of spaghetti, then turned back to the salad greens she had been tearing into a large bowl. "We're not eating fancy tonight," she said, "but we'll make up for it tomorrow. The Easter ham's ready to go into the oven. I made dozens of those rolls you and Darren always liked, Peter. And that fruit and marshmallow and whipped cream salad."

Peter sniffed appreciatively. "I smell chocolate cake too."

Megan's mom rolled out another pie crust and fit it into a pan. "It's in the oven." She smiled at Peter and Megan. "What do you think? Will these three pies plus the cake be enough?"

"I could eat that much right now!" Peter rubbed his stomach.

"Wash your hands, then. You can set the table for supper."

Megan told them that Peter had agreed to help dye eggs. Aunt Gladys handed her a kettle. "You can let the eggs cook while we eat."

The timer went off. Aunt Gladys stopped what she was doing to test the cake in the oven with a toothpick. The toothpick came out clean. "Done!" she said, and set the cake layers on racks to cool. "We'll eat early tomorrow," she planned aloud. "We always have juice and rolls at the church after the sunrise service, but that's not a very big breakfast to last through the morning."

"I've never been to a sunrise service," Megan told her, filling the kettle with cold water. "Do you really get up before sunrise?"

"We sure do. Just like the women who went to Jesus' tomb early on Sunday morning after He was crucified. I still get goosebumps every time I see that Easter morning sun come over the hills and remember what happened that first Easter."

As she lowered the eggs one by one into the water, Megan thought about the weeping women at the tomb and their joy when they realized that Jesus was alive. She turned on the heat beneath the pan, wondering if the Salinas family knew about Jesus. Again, she wished she knew a way *she* could help them.

After a pleasant meal, Megan mixed colored dyes in the old cups Aunt Gladys gave her. "All right, Peter, it's payback time."

Uncle Martin grinned. They heard him telling the adults what had happened in the orchard.

Peter dipped an egg into a cup of purple dye and rolled it gently to keep the color even. "I used to love to do this with my mother when I was little," he said. "Even though I never liked boiled eggs."

"I don't really like them either," Megan replied. "But like I said, it's tradition. I wonder what the Salinas kids will do for Easter."

After they'd rinsed their egg-dying utensils and piled the colored eggs into a basket, they joined the adults around the table for a game of Scrabble. After a while, Uncle Martin excused himself to go outside. When he came back in a few minutes later, he looked worried. He snapped on the TV set but left the volume down. "Low clouds moving in, and it's getting cold," he said. "I'd better listen to the weather report."

The game got loud and exciting. Megan thought no more about Uncle Martin's concern until the older man went over to the television and turned it up. All voices hushed as everyone's attention turned to the meteorologist and his weather map on the screen.

"You orchardists in the upper valley, hook up your frost alarms tonight. A temperature inversion is developing; freezing likely in low-lying areas toward morning ..."

Uncle Martin turned the set off. "I'd better get some sleep," he said. "If it does freeze, it's going to be a long night, especially since I haven't found a replacement for my foreman."

"We'd better all turn in," Peter's dad suggested. "Be sure to wake me if the frost alarm goes off."

Megan went out with Peter to put Jiggs to bed on the enclosed back porch, then helped him haul in the duffel bags with everyone's clothes. They brought in sleeping bags and air mattresses for themselves.

Later, when the house was quiet, Megan raised her head from her bed on the living room floor. "I wonder if the Salinas family stays warm in that van at night."

"I hope so," Peter answered sleepily from across the room.

His words were the last thing she heard until she was roused from a deep sleep by voices in the kitchen.

"It's already freezing in the lower orchards and dropping fast here at the house," she heard Uncle Martin say. "Too fast for us to keep ahead of, I'm afraid."

"I can help." That voice was her mother's.

Megan sat up and reached for her clothes. Peter stirred. "What's a matter?" he mumbled.

"Get dressed," Megan whispered. She grabbed her shoes and stepped across Peter on her way to the kitchen. The two men were pulling on heavy sweaters, jackets, and caps. Uncle Martin's face was creased with worry. Aunt Gladys had just filled the coffeemaker with water and plugged it in.

"We want to help too," Megan said.

"Megan, it's 2:00 A.M.!" Aunt Gladys said.

"That's all right. Isn't there something we can do?"

Peter appeared in the doorway behind her. Uncle Martin looked at them, and some of the creases smoothed away.

"Yes, I think there is," he said.

Apple Orchard Easter

Megan flashed her light over the trunks of the nearby trees, searching for one of the thermometers that Uncle Martin had hung in the orchard.

"I found one!" She pushed up the sleeves of the man's yellow raincoat she wore over her own jacket. The raincoat was a nuisance now, but Darren had said she'd need it when the sprinklers came on. She turned the thermometer toward the beam of her flashlight. "It's 34 degrees."

"Cold enough to turn on the sprinklers," her stepfather answered. "I hope the gang in the lower orchard gets the smudge pots lit in time."

"The gang" consisted of Megan's mom, Peter, and Uncle Martin. Lighting the smudge pots was a dirty, smelly job that Megan had gladly postponed in favor of helping Darren with the sprinklers. She swung her light from side to side as she followed him down the long aisle of trees. The frigid air stung her cheeks and made her nose drip. "How far to the pond?"

"Almost there. I hope the pump won't give me trouble. I must have been your age the last time I touched a pump like that."

Megan tried to imagine her distinguished-looking stepfather at her age. Grown-ups always seemed so ... in charge, although she knew that in this crisis, the adults were worried. A hard freeze could obliterate the Wirths' whole yearly income in a single night and would surely give the big company that wanted to take over their land extra leverage.

At the far edge of the orchard, Darren led the way downhill. He continued, "I used to stay with Uncle Martin and Aunt Gladys during spring vacations just like we're doing now. Once we worked for three nights fighting a cold spell. They lost a good part of their crop that year."

His flashlight caught the gleam of water in the blackness ahead. "There's the pond," he said. He shone the light on a small building. "Here's the well house. Water pumped from the well fills the pond. Sprinkler systems use a lot of water."

"I suppose that's why we saw smudge pots or fans in so many orchards."

"Right, though some people want to see smudge pots outlawed because they pollute the air." He flashed his light back at the pond. "What's going on! The pond should be brim full!"

The water's black surface was now a couple of feet below last summer's dried grasses, which marked the usual pond level. Darren stepped closer. His light moved around the pond's rim and stopped. "There's the problem," he said. "A washout." They both stared at the break in the earthen berm that was supposed to dam the water. "Probably rockchucks digging," he said.

"Is there enough water left to ice the trees?" Megan asked.

"We'll have to pray there is. Otherwise, we're in big trouble." He stooped at the edge of the pond to inspect the second pump that fed pond water into the underground lines which ran through the orchard. "This looks okay, anyhow."

Megan held her light so he could see to unscrew the intake hose from the pump. "It's been lying here all winter. I'd better make sure mice haven't built nests in it." He lifted the other end of the hose above his head and shook it. Sticks and debris rattled onto the ground.

He refastened the hose to the pump and adjusted the screening over the free end. "The screen was bent back just far enough for the mice to squeeze in," he told Megan. "Here, see if the hose will reach the water while I try the pump."

She tugged the free end of the hose down the bank and dropped it into the pond. If the water level went down much farther, the hose would be sucking air.

The motor sputtered and choked, then started. "We'll wait a few minutes for the water to get into the lines," Darren said. "Meanwhile, I'll start the well pump to get water flowing into the pond. Then we need to check each sprinkler to be sure it's working."

Megan shoved her hands up opposite sleeves of the stiff yellow raincoat and hugged herself. Now that she'd stopped moving, the cold seeped through her layers of clothes. "What will we do if we run out of water in the pond?"

"We'll have to see if we can beg or borrow smudge pots, I guess. As Uncle Martin would say, 'We'll do our best and trust God for the rest.' "

Megan grinned. "Were Uncle Martin and Aunt Gladys as nice when you were young as they are now?" she asked.

"They never change." She heard the smile in her stepfather's reply. "Even when they lost so much of their crop that time, they just said God would look out for them. They were the ones ..." he paused, remembering. "When I was very young, they were the ones who first told me why Jesus came. Uncle Martin said that even if I had been the only person on earth, Jesus would still have come to take the punishment for my sins because He loved me so much."

Megan listened, thinking of the time after her father had left them. Her mother had found strength in her faith, but it took Megan a long time to understand that God wasn't punishing her for some wrongdoing by taking her daddy away. She hadn't wanted her mother to marry again, but now she felt grateful for Darren and his leadership in their family.

A whispering spread through the orchard. The sprinklers began to spray mist over the surrounding trees. As Megan pulled a rain hat from her pocket and put it on over her cap, she shined her light once more toward the break in the dam. The rockchuck that had so interested Jiggs earlier that day had dug tunnels, not trenches. "I'd like to take a closer look at that washout," she told Darren.

"Be careful, it will be muddy. I'll start checking the sprinklers." He moved off into the darkness.

Megan followed the top of the berm until she came to the washout. With her beam of light, she traced the muddy pathway left by the escaping water. A little stream still dribbled through the cut and down the hillside. A rockchuck could have tunneled into the dam, she supposed. The pressure of the pond could have caused water to flood through the tunnel and erode the bank like this. But the bottom of the washout was at least four feet below the top of the dam. Wouldn't water seeping through a tunnel that far down just make it collapse upon itself? And if that had happened, most of the pond water should still be there.

Oh well. She shrugged and retraced her steps to the edge of the orchard. Darren thought a rockchuck was responsible. He was probably right, but the memory of the trespassers nagged at the back of her thoughts.

She walked up and down the long aisles of trees, shining her light on the overhead nozzles to be sure each one turned freely and spun out the water that would cover each twig and bud in a protective coat of ice. She could see Darren's light moving through the orchard several rows up.

She stopped to check one of the orchard thermometers. Already a thin film of ice encased it. "It's down to 32," she called to him.

"We were just in time. We'd better hurry. The others will need help with the smudge pots."

When all of the sprinklers were inspected, Megan and Darren walked to the ranch house and clumped into the back entry. Jiggs lifted his head as if to ask what they were doing up in the middle of the night, then curled up again. They hung their rain gear on hooks and slipped out of their muddy boots.

Aunt Gladys handed them hot cocoa as they came into the kitchen. "I made both coffee and cocoa for you to carry to the others, but take a moment to warm up before you leave," she said. Megan pulled off her wet gloves and cupped her hands around the warm mug, sipping gratefully.

Aunt Gladys handed her another pair of gloves. "I wish I could go along to help, but somebody has to stay here at the house in case Martin calls. Like just now—he called on the cell phone in his truck. They need all the help they can get."

"We're on our way." Darren Lewis gulped the last of his cocoa and set the mug on the counter. He quickly told Aunt Gladys about the low water in the pond. "Can you watch the sprinklers?"

"I'll watch them," Gladys said. "If they stop, I'll go turn off the pump."

Megan got back into her boots and borrowed yellow mackintosh and helped carry the thermoses of coffee and cocoa out to the minivan. Diamonds winked from the iced branches as the headlights swept the orchard's edge. They turned onto the main road where the pickup trucks of other orchardists sped back and forth.

In the first of Uncle Martin's lower orchards, smudge pots belched flame and filled the air with acrid smoke. The minivan bumped along a dirt road as Megan peered down the rows of trees, looking for the rest of the family.

"They've finished here," Darren said.

In the next orchard, smudge pots burned in the distance. Black shapes flitted past their glow—Mom and

Peter working their way up every other row, lighting pots by every other tree. Uncle Martin checked the unlit pots, refilling some of them from a tank of diesel fuel on the truck.

Darren parked the minivan. Carrying the hot drinks, he and Megan hurried to meet the others. Flames shooting from a smudge pot's chimney made a circle of light and warmth. Megan laughed when her mother and Peter came into the light. Their faces, hands, and clothing were smeared with soot.

Peter helped himself to cocoa while Megan poured coffee for the adults. "Just wait," he told her. "You'll be as dirty as we are before we're done."

"The sprinklers are all working fine, Uncle Martin," Darren said. "How's it going here?"

"We're doing our best," he answered wearily. "Only the Lord knows if our best will be enough. It's below freezing, and we've still got this orchard and another one to finish."

Megan opened her mouth to tell about the washout at the pond, but Darren caught her eye and shook his head. "With Megan and me helping, can we do it?" he asked.

"I wish I could say yes ..."

The older man looked very tired, and Megan realized her stepfather didn't want to burden him further. Then inspiration hit her. "Uncle Martin," she interrupted. "Remember Mr. Salinas and Luis? Couldn't they help?"

45

He pushed back his cap and rubbed his nose. "Good thinking, Megan! They'd be a big help. And they need work. Darren, will you go see if they'll come?"

"I've not met Mr. Salinas," Peter's dad said. "One of you kids had better come along."

"I'll go," Megan said. "They'd never recognize Peter with that sooty face!"

At the campground, the Salinas family's van was still parked among the willows. Frost glistened on it in the glare of their headlights. Newspapers covered the insides of the windows.

Megan slipped out of the minivan and tapped softly on the door of the battered van. Someone stirred inside. She tapped again and called, "Mr. Salinas, it's Megan Parnell."

She heard low voices inside the van, then the door slid part way open, and Carlos Salinas stepped out. In his hand he clutched a short, heavy stick. He squinted in the headlights.

"Ah." The man's eyes lit up as he recognized Megan. He dropped the stick back inside the doorway. "What is it, amiga?"

"My uncle, Martin Wirth, asks if you and Luis would come and help us with the smudge pots."

Mr. Salinas glanced toward the minivan. "That's my stepfather in there," Megan said. "Can you come? Now?"

"Sí, sí." A broad smile spread across his face. "Un momento." He poked his head back into the van and spoke softly. Someone handed his jacket out the door. "Luis comes," he said as he put the coat on.

Long hours later, Megan walked once more through the upper orchard. Her aching feet crunched through ice-coated grass blades. Water dripped from her rain hat, and mist whirling from the nozzles overhead slicked her raincoat. She couldn't remember ever feeling so exhausted.

She glanced up to check the next sprinkler. It had stopped turning. The pond must have run dry! At the same time she realized she no longer needed the flashlight. The blackness overhead had grayed while she struggled to stay awake; now the sky filled with a colorless light. A few stars shrank to pinpricks and disappeared. Stars! That meant the clouds that had held the cold air close to the ground had gone too.

She hurried to the end of the row and looked for the thermometer she knew was nearby. "Thirty-four," she said aloud. "It's going up! Thank You, Lord. Apples, you're saved!"

She gazed into the branches silhouetted against the sky and caught her breath at the glistening fringes of ice hanging from each branch and twig. Icicles—thousands and millions of icicles.

Darren came out of the orchard, far up the hill, and shouted that he would turn off the pump. At that moment the ranch truck growled up the driveway. Uncle Martin, with Peter and Mom in the cab beside him, pulled up and gestured for her to hop onto the tailgate.

She slid off when the truck stopped in the yard. Aunt Gladys and Jiggs came out to greet them.

"We did it, Uncle Martin, didn't we?" Peter exulted, his teeth flashing white against his soot-blackened face. "We saved the crop!"

"We won't know for sure until the blooms come out. But I think so. With God's help and yours, I think so."

Megan looked around at the tired, dirty group. "Where're Mr. Salinas and Luis?"

"They're extinguishing the smudge pots. I'll go back in a while, pay them, and take them home. I'm glad you thought of them, Megan. Their help made all the difference. They're hard workers, both of them."

"We couldn't have gotten along without any of these dear folks," said Aunt Gladys. "We'll miss this morning's sunrise service, but your Easter breakfast is ready. Then you each deserve a good hot shower and some sleep."

Easter! Megan wondered if the Salinas family would have any special treats to celebrate the day. "Do you think we have enough food to send some home with Luis and his dad?"

"Of course," agreed Aunt Gladys.

"The kids could have the eggs we colored," Peter offered.

"We could send some of the ham and a pie," Megan's mother added. "And some rolls and a salad."

"I'm sure they'll appreciate that," Uncle Martin said. "After last night, I can see that we really do need some extra hands on the ranch. I'm going to offer Carlos a job."

A warm glow made Megan forget the chill of the morning as she thought of Rosalía and her brothers and sisters. She grinned at Peter. If Carlos went to work for

Uncle Martin, maybe the family could move out of their cold, crowded van into a real home.

The group started toward the house.

"Look, everybody! The sun's coming up!" Peter pointed toward the eastern hills. They watched as a few cloud streaks flamed pink and apricot. A crescent of melted gold pushed above the horizon. Shadows spilled down the hills ahead of the light as the sun rolled into the sky.

"Oh, look at the rainbows," Megan exclaimed. "The orchard's full of rainbows!" The rising sun struck through the millions of icicles, splintering the rays into all the colors of light.

Uncle Martin straightened his shoulders and smiled. "It's Easter morning," he exclaimed. "Christ is risen!"

Together they chorused the answer of the early Christians, "He is risen indeed!"

Getting Acquainted

After the family returned home, the months flew by. Peter and Megan finished the school year and enjoyed a busy summer. In September, they began their junior year at Madrona Bay High School.

Occasionally, Peter's father called the Wirths, so they knew the Salinas family now lived in the old ranch house near Uncle Martin and Aunt Gladys. They knew the big company was still pressuring the Wirths to sell their property. In the latest telephone conversation, Uncle Martin had said that they were expecting a bumper crop, despite some frost damage from last spring. The apples were almost ready to pick.

"Can't we go to Yakima again?" Peter asked.

"Harvest time's the busiest season for farmers," his father answered. "They wouldn't appreciate company now."

No more was said, but on the following Thursday evening the telephone rang while Megan and Peter were doing homework in the kitchen. Megan answered. "For you or Darren, Mom," she called. "It's Aunt Gladys."

Sarah came to the phone, and Megan returned to her work. She and Peter both looked up when Megan's mom exclaimed, "Oh, no, Aunt Gladys! How did it happen?"

51

Sarah listened, her face showing concern. She nodded, then said, "Tomorrow? Aunt Gladys, we'll all be praying. Please call and let us know how the surgery goes."

Darren came into the kitchen. "What's wrong, Sarah?"

"Uncle Martin got hurt. He was in the orchard with some workers. The driver jumped off the tractor and left the engine running. Somehow it slipped out of gear and knocked Uncle Martin under the wheels. Thank the Lord, the dirt was soft and Carlos and Luis Salinas were able to get him free. He might have been killed!" She paused. "He's to have back surgery tomorrow. The doctor says he won't be able to work for several months."

"What about the apple harvest?" Peter asked. "This is the worst possible time for him to get hurt."

"You're right about that," Darren said. He sat down to think. "You know that couple weeks' vacation I was saving for our Arizona trip at Christmas? If the rest of you wouldn't be too disappointed, I could take it now and go help at the ranch."

"We can go to Arizona some other time," Sarah said. "It's hard to get long-term substitute librarians or I'd take time off too."

"I always wanted to try apple picking," Peter said. "Couldn't I take my assignments along and go with you, Dad?"

The thought made Megan prick up her ears. Though she'd looked forward to seeing Arizona this winter, to spend these beautiful fall days outdoors in the sunshine sounded almost as good.

After much discussion, the family decided that if Peter and Megan could clear it with their teachers, they too would go to Yakima, enroll in school there temporarily, and help on the ranch after school.

By Sunday, Peter, his dad, and Megan were in Yakima. That afternoon, Megan jogged beside Peter down the Wirths' long driveway toward the Salinas' house. They passed endless rows of trees hanging heavy with big red apples.

"Remember the icicles on these trees last spring?" Peter asked.

"I'll never forget it," Megan replied. "I couldn't believe at first that coating the trees with ice would keep them from freezing, but it worked." She drew in a deep breath of crisp fall air. "Just smell those apples!"

Peter sniffed. "Mm-hmm!" He changed the subject. "Poor Uncle Martin looked miserable in that hospital bed."

"I know," said Megan. "The doctors said his back surgery went well, but I'll bet he won't be able to work for a long time. He's got to be worried about getting his crop in. And that big conglomerate is hovering like a vulture, hoping he'll give in and sell. I heard Aunt Gladys tell your dad that one of their officials had been there again the morning of the accident."

"Well, we're here to help all we can. And he has the Salinas family. He said Mr. Salinas is one of the best workers he ever hired."

As they rounded a bend, three dark-haired children playing beside the road looked up.

"Here they come!" Teodoro Salinas shouted. He scampered along the dusty roadway toward Megan and Peter. When he reached them, he grabbed one hand of each and skipped along between them. "I'm 5!" he said proudly.

"We know. Happy birthday, Teodoro." Peter tousled the boy's hair. "Have you had any more falls into the river?"

The little boy giggled. "Mamacita says, no more river."

The girls came up. Alicia, the older, smiled shyly. Isabel took Megan's other hand and craned around to look at Peter. "Where is your dog?"

"Jiggs? He's up at the ranch house with my dad."

"Can I play with him sometime?"

"Sure thing."

Megan dropped Isabel's hand for a moment while she adjusted her camera's neckstrap to a more comfortable position, then patted her pocket to be sure she'd brought an extra roll of film. They had already returned from the hospital in town by the time Mrs. Salinas sent Rosalía to invite them to supper, so they had no birthday present for Teodoro. But Megan could offer to take pictures of his party.

They turned onto the short drive leading to the old ranch house. It no longer looked deserted. A couple of well-used bicycles leaned against the porch, curtains fluttered at the windows, and good smells drifted through the open front door.

"Peter! Megan! Welcome to our home." Rosalía scooped up fat little Juan as he toddled ahead of her onto the porch. Her dark eyes sparkled, and her cheeks were as rosy as the baby's.

"Mamacita, they are here! Teodoro, Alicia, Isabel, bring our guests inside."

Magdalena Salinas came from the kitchen, smiling and nodding and wiping her hands on a towel.

"I happy you here," she said to them, straining to think of the right English words. "Teodoro ... he birthday now because of you."

"She means if you hadn't saved him from the river, he would not be here for his birthday," said Rosalía, beaming at Peter.

"Thank you for inviting us to his party, Mrs. Salinas," Megan said.

Magdalena smiled at her and said something in Spanish to the children. Rosalía handed Juan to Isabel, and the four younger children disappeared to wash for supper. "Come in," Rosalía said. "Everything is almost ready."

They followed her and her mother into the old-fashioned farm kitchen. Bright paper flowers hung from the light fixture above the big table. A colorful piñata in the shape of a pony stood on a sideboard with a few packages piled beside it.

"Rosalía," Megan said, "we didn't have time to buy a present for Teodoro, but I brought my camera. Ask your mother if she would like me to take some pictures."

Rosalía translated, and Magdalena smiled. "¡Sí! Gracias."

Megan snapped a picture of the piñata and one of Mrs. Salinas and Rosalía at the stove.

Just then Luis and his father came through the back door. Carlos greeted the visitors as enthusiastically as his wife had done. Luis stood in the background, his black eyes revealing little expression. He studied Megan's camera.

"You see Señor Wirth?" Carlos asked. "He is okay?"

"His back hurts," Peter said, "but he wants to come home and work. The doctor says he can't—not yet."

"He no worry. You ..." Carlos pointed to Peter and Megan, "and my families ..." He gestured around the kitchen. "We take care of apples until he well."

"We were glad you and Luis were there when he had the accident," Megan said, smiling toward Rosalía's twin.

Luis did not smile back. "No accident," he muttered.

"What do you mean?" Megan asked. "Uncle Martin said the tractor slipped out of gear."

Luis shrugged and turned away. His father urged them toward the table. Mrs. Salinas took a steaming pan from the oven and set it on a mat. Luis' dark face warmed with his first smile since he'd entered the house. "Enchiladas! My favorite!"

Rosalía dished beans into one bowl, reddish rice into another. She set them on the table and went to call the younger children.

"Please, sit. Sit," urged Carlos as Teodoro and the others came into the kitchen.

Teodoro saw the big paper flowers above the table and grinned. Then he caught sight of the sideboard. His eyes grew big. "Piñata!" he squealed. "A piñata for my birthday!"

"For after supper," Rosalía told him, laughing. "The girls and I made it in the evenings after he was in bed," she said to Peter and Megan as she sat down.

The Salinas family all bowed their heads and made the sign of the cross. Carlos Salinas recited a blessing in Spanish, and they crossed themselves again. Megan quickly ducked her head and gave thanks for the food too.

They passed their plates to Mr. Salinas, who served the enchiladas—corn tortillas rolled around a filling of shredded meat and baked with a topping of spicy sauce. Megan slipped out of her chair for a moment to take a shot of the family around the table.

"Everything looks delicious!" she said to Mrs. Salinas as she sat down again.

"Gracias." Magdalena smiled. She put a bowl of food and a spoon on little Juan's high-chair tray and asked her guests a question in Spanish.

Rosalía translated. "Why didn't your mother come with you, Megan?"

"She couldn't leave her job," Megan answered. "She's a school librarian."

Magdalena listened closely, her lips pursed, and clucked her tongue in sympathy.

"But Peter and I can stay for a couple of weeks, at least," Megan said.

"No school?" Carlos asked.

Megan passed her plate for another enchilada. She thought of their rush to get everything arranged after Aunt Gladys had called Thursday evening, including getting excused from classes.

"Our teachers gave us projects to work on, but we're going to go to school here too. Aunt Gladys told us about the special evening classes for kids who work during the day."

"Oh, isn't that great, Luis?" Rosalía said. "We can all go to school together."

Luis concentrated on scooping up his last bite of beans and rice. "I should be staying home to work."

Mr. Salinas looked hard at his son. He spoke sternly. "My children must study. Someday have good, steady jobs."

Luis frowned at his plate. "Sí, papá," he answered.

Rosalía hopped up to help her mother remove the plates.

"Piñata now?" Teodoro squirmed hopefully in his chair.

"Not yet, niño." Mrs. Salinas took a platter of flat, sugar-and-cinnamon coated pastries from a cupboard and brought them to the table.

Teodoro and Isabel clapped their hands. "¡Sopapillas!"

Peter took a bite of his crispy pastry. "Mmmm. Is this Mexican birthday cake?"

"You could say that," Rosalía said. "Mamá makes them whenever we have a birthday."

Teodoro grinned from ear to ear as he nibbled the edge of a big sopapilla. Megan laughed and snapped a picture of him across the table. As she glanced away, she caught a smolder of resentment in Luis' dark eyes. What was wrong with him, anyway? But when the whole family trooped into the living room, Luis joined in the fun.

He tacked a cord from the top of the door across the room to the top of a window. Then he took the pony piñata, covered with many colors of fringed tissue paper, and hung it from the cord so it dangled above Teodoro's head in the center of the room.

The little boy clapped his hands and danced about.

"Everybody gets two swings," said Luis. "Teodoro first. It is his birthday." He put a stick in his brother's hands.

Rosalía blindfolded the child and turned him around a couple of times.

"Swing," everybody shouted.

The little boy swung in the wrong direction. He swung again so hard that he lost his balance and sat down on the floor. He pulled the blindfold off and laughed along with the rest of them.

All of the younger children got a turn, even little Juan, whom Rosalía held in her arms as he tried to hit the piñata.

Then it was Teodoro's turn again. This time the stick landed with a smack on the piñata. The papier-mâché broke open, showering candies and small toys. The children scrambled to pick them up. While the family laughed and called encouragement, Megan snapped pictures.

Afterward, Peter and Megan thanked Mrs. Salinas for dinner and once more wished Teodoro happy birthday.

Rosalía walked out onto the porch with them while Luis watched from the doorway.

"We'll see you in the orchard in the morning," Peter said.

"Good," Rosalía answered. "We can pick together."

"Do we need to bring anything?" Megan asked.

"Wear a hat," Rosalía said. "And bring your own picking sacks."

"Picking sacks?" Megan questioned. Luis only lifted an eyebrow, but that was enough to convey his scorn.

Rosalía caught the look. "How is she to know, Luis?" she scolded her brother. "Ask Mrs. Wirth," she said to Megan. "She will give them to you."

Smarting, but determined to extend an olive branch to Luis, Megan said, "I've never picked apples before. Luis, will you show us how?"

"I will show you. But it takes more than a couple of weeks to become a good picker."

"Fine," she said, pretending not to notice the boy's patronizing attitude. "We'll do the best we can. And then we'll have to get used to going to school at night. I'm glad we already know you two." Megan couldn't read Luis' black eyes.

"Yeah. Well, you'll find the norteamericanos don't spend much time with us latinos." He nodded a curt good night and went back into the house.

Rosalía looked after her brother, a frown creasing her forehead. "I don't know what's the matter with Luis. He's not usually like this."

"Don't worry about it, Rosalía," Megan said. "We had a wonderful time at the party. I'm glad we'll be seeing lots of you in the next couple of weeks."

But as she and Peter trudged up the hill to Aunt Gladys' house, she wondered what they'd done to make Luis so angry. And why had he said Uncle Martin's injury was no accident?

Apples Everywhere

The sun wasn't even up next morning when Megan heard voices outside. She looked out the guest bedroom window to see her stepfather in the drive beside the orchard talking to several men and a few women. "Better hurry," she said to herself. "The pickers are ready to start." She noticed that Carlos Salinas was in the group, but she didn't see Luis or Rosalía.

She threw on jeans, a T-shirt, and a sweatshirt and hurried to the kitchen. Peter was already eating. Aunt Gladys dished up a big bowl of oatmeal and set it before her.

Aunt Gladys poured herself a cup of coffee. "Darren's taking to this job as if he's been in the orchard business all his life," she said to them. "With Carlos supervising the pickers and Darren taking care of the other details, Martin can just relax and get well."

"I hope so," Megan answered. She wondered if she should bring up Luis' remark about the accident but decided to say nothing that might cause the Wirths extra concern.

"How are you two doing?" Aunt Gladys carried her cup to the table and sat down across from Peter and Megan. "This is a big day for you—starting new jobs and a new school at the same time."

63

Megan glanced at Peter. "I'm a little nervous," she admitted. "It's not like we'll be here that long, but still ... I wonder if we can keep up with the other pickers. And will the kids at school like us, and can we find our classes—that sort of thing."

"Don't worry. You know the Lord will be right there beside you. Do you want me to drive you to school this first afternoon?"

"Thank you," Megan answered. "But we can go with Rosalía and Luis. They'll show us around."

"But first we have a full shift of apple picking," Peter said. He carried his dishes to the sink, rinsed them, and put them in the dishwasher.

The kitchen clock showed barely 7:00 A.M. when they grabbed their hats, called good-bye to Aunt Gladys, and hurried out the back door, carrying the folded nylon picking bags she'd given them. Jiggs bounced at the end of his rope. Peter hugged his dog and unfastened the rope. "I'll tie him to a tree while we pick."

"Forgot my camera," Megan said. "Wait for me." She dashed back to her bedroom, checked to be sure she had film, then slung the camera around her neck. Snapshots of the harvesters would add to the chances of an A on her report for her Madrona High teachers.

As they started across the drive, they saw Luis and Rosalía heading toward them and stopped to wait. Rosalía's long hair hung in two braids over her shoulders. Brother and sister both wore battered cloth hats. Jiggs dashed to meet them and escorted them up the hill.

Luis frowned at Megan's camera. "Do you carry that everywhere you go?"

"No," she answered. "But taking pictures is my hobby."

Luis shrugged. "Rich kid's hobby," he muttered under his breath.

A sharp retort leaped to the tip of Megan's tongue, but she shut her mouth to hold it back. Explaining her school project wouldn't change this opinionated boor's mind.

Peter glanced from one to the other but said nothing. He lifted the strap of his picking sack over his head, as Luis and Rosalía had done, and let it hang at his waist. A metal rim held its top open. The bottom of the long canvas bag folded up against the front of the rim, held there by knotted cords threaded through metal hooks.

"See," said Rosalía, showing him how to release the cords. "You can change the length of the bag by moving the knots. When it's full, you just let the apples roll out the open bottom into the bin."

"Slowly," Luis said. "If the apples come out too fast and hard, they will bruise."

A farm tractor with a forklift attached to the front came down the hill toward them. Peter's dad stood behind the driver, who stopped the tractor to let him jump off.

"Here's the rest of our crew! Are you ready for work?"

"Hi, Dad," Peter answered. "Ready and willing!"

Darren Lewis introduced Megan and Peter to the ruddy-faced man on the tractor. "This is Scud Sawyer," he said. "He'll pick up the bins with the forklift after you fill them."

They said hello. Scud Sawyer nodded as if he had more important things on his mind than a bunch of kids. Something about the man's red face and thick neck seemed familiar to Megan.

"Your dad's about six rows up," Darren said to Luis and Rosalía. "He'll tell you all where he wants you to pick."

He hopped back on the tractor. It moved on, and the four started along the aisle of trees he'd indicated.

"Funny," said Peter. "I think I've seen that Scud Sawyer before."

"Maybe you have. He was at the packing plant the day you two and Mr. Wirth gave papá and me a ride," Luis said.

"You're right!" Megan said. "I remember now. He's the guy who called you names and was just plain nasty."

"What's he doing here?" Peter asked.

"You tell me." Luis muttered the words under his breath in the habit that was beginning to irk Megan.

"What do you mean by that?" she asked sharply.

"Mr. Wirth hired him several weeks ago," Rosalía interceded. "He's rude to the pickers. Luis doesn't trust him."

"I know Uncle Martin didn't see what happened at the packing plant," Peter said. "He'd never have hired him. Do you think Scud Sawyer remembers you and your dad?"

"Probably not," Luis answered. "He's like most gringos. He thinks all mexicanos look alike."

The bitterness in his voice disturbed Megan and irritated her too. Luis was doing the same thing he said "gringos" did: lumping a whole group of people together. And she didn't like being called a gringo.

"If that's what Mr. Sawyer thinks, he's not very smart," Rosalía said, trying to smooth over the tense moment.

They passed many wooden boxes, about four feet square by two feet high, sitting in the aisle between the trees. Some were filled, or partly filled, with apples. Their crisp fragrance hung in the air.

"Hello, papá!" cried Rosalía.

Carlos Salinas straightened from inspecting the apples in a bin. Though the air felt chilly, he was already perspiring. Pushing back his straw hat, he wiped his face with the bandanna he wore around his neck. "You bring friends to pick, sí?" He smiled and patted Jiggs. "This one too?"

"No," Peter said. "He's going to watch."

Mr. Salinas spoke in Spanish to the twins. "He says for us to show you what to do," explained Rosalía.

A man climbed down a ladder in a nearby tree and emptied his full bag into a bin. "Each person puts his tag on his bin," she told them, pointing to the man's cardboard tag. "He keeps the stub to prove how many bins he's picked. Good pickers can fill 12 or 13 bins a day."

The man leaned into the bin with his picking sack, opened the end, and let the apples roll gently onto the ones already in the box. Though the light was still dim, Megan snapped a picture. The man looked surprised, then grinned.

Luis watched but said nothing. He got tags from his dad and wrote their names on them. "We're supposed to take the next two trees," he said, pointing to two on which the red fruit hung heavy under leaves wet with dew.

He reached up to a nearby branch and showed them how to twist the apples from their stems. "Pick with both hands. Faster that way."

"Pick all the apples," Rosalía said. "The ones that are too small or have blemishes will be sorted out for the juice factory."

Luis demonstrated how to lean the ladders into openings among the boughs and position them so they were safe to climb. Then he and Rosalía went to the other tree, leaving Megan and Peter to climb their ladders and get started.

"I'm getting water down my neck," Peter called from the other side of the tree.

"Me too, and it's cold." Megan grasped the limb her ladder leaned against and reached for the nearest apple. She dropped it gently into her bag. Apples, apples everywhere. "They smell so good, I'd rather eat them than pick them," she said. She aimed her camera at some particularly perfect apples framed against the brightening sky.

Her sleeves were wet but her bag was almost full when Peter appeared at the foot of her ladder. He patted Jiggs. "I'm ready to empty my sack," he said. "Want me to take a picture of you picking?"

"Sure," Megan answered, handing the camera down to him. She plucked a couple of apples and held them above her bag as if dropping them in. When he snapped the picture, she put them in the bag and climbed awkwardly down the ladder.

"Whew! These bags are heavy when they're full!"

"Megan, why don't we give the apples we pick to Rosalía and Luis?" Peter suggested.

Megan thought about the telephoto lens she wanted for her camera. The apples she'd pick in the next couple of weeks would easily pay for it. Besides, Luis had been nothing but a pain. But whatever the twins earned went to help their family. She could keep saving from her allowance for the lens. "All right," she agreed.

She followed Peter over to Rosalía's and Luis' bins. "Look," she said. "They're already ahead of us."

She leaned over the side of the bin and tried to roll her apples out without bruising them.

"What are you doing?" Luis had come up behind with another full sack. "Your bins are over there."

"You've already picked *two* sacks?" Megan exclaimed, ignoring what he said. "You're going to leave us way behind!"

"We will if you do not even know which bin has your name on it," he answered scornfully.

"We know this is yours," Megan said, her temper rising. Go slowly, she warned herself. How would Jesus handle an irritating guy like this?

Megan tilted her head to the side and made herself smile at him. "We're embarrassed we pick so slowly. If you let us put our apples in your bins, then the other pickers won't tease us."

A grudging little smile lifted the corners of Luis' mouth. "Okay, if it makes you feel better," he said.

They went back to picking. Megan was pleased at the tiny hint of thawing in Luis' attitude, even if he hadn't been exactly gracious in what he'd said. The sun shone through openings between the boughs, warming the cool air. Soon she was thankful for her hat, even though the limbs kept knocking it askew.

Sweat trickled down her face, and her sweatshirt had dried by the time they'd filled the two bins. Her neck and shoulders ached, and her mouth felt parched. She picked the last apple within reach and descended the ladder. "Hi, Boy," she said to Jiggs. "It's time to move this ladder to another spot."

She emptied her bag, then wrestled the ladder to another section of the tree. Luis, who was also emptying a bag, watched her for a moment, then returned to his work.

She climbed to her new spot and began to pick. The ladder shifted under her weight, lifting away from the supporting branch. "Oops," she muttered. "I'd better get down and slant it more." But she decided to wait until her bag was full.

She wiped sweat from her eyes. Her legs trembled with weariness. Not a breath of air stirred the leaves. She twisted her upper body to reach for more apples.

Suddenly something jarred the ladder. Blindly, she grabbed for a branch.

Some Days
You Just Can't Win

Her foot slipped off the rung and groped desperately for something solid. Then, as the ladder flopped back against the limb that supported it, her foot found the rung. With knees too weak to hold her, she leaned against the ladder and looked down.

Luis stared up at her, a teasing glint in his eyes. "You can use your camera to take a picture of a bad accident if you don't brace your ladder better," he said.

Fury flooded over her panic. He had deliberately bumped the ladder just to scare her! She didn't even try to control the sarcasm in her voice. "Thanks for telling me," she said. "You're a real gentleman."

His face turned a deep, embarrassed red. Satisfied, she watched him hunch his shoulders and walk away. Gradually her anger faded. She remembered his teasing expression as he looked up at her. Maybe he hadn't intended to be mean. What if she'd just ruined whatever progress she'd made in overcoming his resentment of them?

The tractor growled through the orchard and stopped somewhere close by. People called to one another and moved toward it. Megan looked down to see Aunt Gladys' white curls.

"Hello, you two! Mr. Sawyer's just brought a cooler of fresh water. Can you stop long enough for a drink?"

"Let me at it," Peter exclaimed, scrambling down his ladder.

"Hi, Aunt Gladys." Megan climbed down too and set her half-full bag on the ground. "How is Uncle Martin today?"

The woman gave them each a paper cup. "According to the nurse I just talked to, he's doing well. I'm going in to see him soon."

Luis and Rosalía emptied full sacks into a new bin. Aunt Gladys offered them cups too.

"Thank you. We have our own." Rosalía pulled a collapsible metal cup from her pocket.

The four accompanied Aunt Gladys to the wooden bench where the big cooler sat. Pickers opened the spigot to run water into their cups, then drank thirstily. Some of them smiled at Megan and Peter and said "Buenos días."

Megan gulped her first cupful without pausing and filled it a second time. Luis hadn't looked at her.

Down the aisle of trees, Scud Sawyer had maneuvered the tines of the forklift into the space between the double floors of a full bin. They watched him move the forklift ahead until the tines passed completely through the space. Then he drove to another full bin and did the same thing with it. The tractor rolled away down the aisle with both boxes.

Megan swallowed the rest of her water. "That was good," she said and smiled toward Luis and his sister. Luis still refused to look at her. He snatched up his empty bag and beckoned to his sister. "Come, Rosalía. We have work to do." He called to his father, who had stopped to check a bin farther down their aisle. "Where next, papá?"

Mr. Salinas pointed to another tree closer to the road. Luis and Rosalía dragged their ladders to the new location.

"I saw what Luis did to your ladder," Peter said as they returned to their picking.

"He's been nothing but a pain," Megan said. "But he wasn't trying to hurt me. And maybe he's got things on his mind we know nothing about."

I'm sure that's true, she mused as she began again to fill her sack. Picking produce is hard work. The pay is low and in lots of migrant families, everybody—mother and children too—has to pick in order for the family to survive. If they want to stay in one place, like the Salinas family, they must find other work when the picking is finished or live on unemployment or welfare. Because they have to move so often, the kids get behind in school. It's hard to hope that life will ever be easier.

Even so, Luis didn't need to be so unpleasant. "Lord Jesus," Megan sighed, "please help me to understand him and treat him the way You want me to."

After a while, Megan searched the branches around her in vain for enough apples to finish filling her bag. She climbed down her ladder. "Peter, I think we're finished with this tree," she called up to her stepbrother.

"I see a few more," he told her. "Be right with you."

She emptied her sack into one of Rosalía and Luis' bins. A young man with muscular brown arms walked past carrying a ladder. Black eyes smiled as he greeted Megan in Spanish.

She smiled back. I wonder where he comes from, she thought. I wonder where he'll go when he's finished with the apple harvest.

Peter climbed down his ladder.

"Peter, I think I know what I'll write about for my project."

"What?" He straightened his back and groaned.

"I'll write about the people who pick the apples."

"Want me to give you my impressions of the job?"

Megan grinned and rubbed her sore neck. "I think they're probably about the same as mine. No, I mean the migrant workers. We can go home in a couple of weeks. But they have to do this all the time."

The day grew hotter and Megan's arms grew heavier, the aches more numerous. By the time they paused to eat their sandwiches, she felt like an apple-picking robot, almost too tired to eat. But the brief rest refreshed her.

Afterwards, she and Peter dragged their ladders to the tree next to where Rosalía and Luis were working and set them in place. At 3:00, Peter called up to Rosalía, "Your last bin is almost full."

"Good," she called back. She climbed down the ladder and carried her sack toward the bin. "It's time to quit and get ready for school."

They all emptied their sacks. Luis collected the stubs of their tags and stalked away to turn them in so they'd get credit for their work. Rosalía watched him go, then turned to Megan and Peter. "Thank you for giving us your apples today. That was very kind of you."

"You're welcome," Megan answered, thinking it wouldn't have hurt Luis to say thank you too. They walked out of the orchard.

On a level area near the ranch buildings, Scud Sawyer had stacked full bins in rows eight long and four high. They watched a truck back a straddle buggy over a row. The driver made the frame inside the buggy come down. Then the rails at the bottom squeezed together and the frame lifted, hoisting all the boxes off the ground. The truck lumbered away with the load.

"How long will the others work?" Megan asked, gesturing toward the dusty cars and pickups the harvesters had arrived in that morning.

"Another two or three hours," Rosalía answered.

"I've noticed that most of the workers are men," Peter said. "I thought whole families came to pick."

"Sometimes they do." Rosalía folded her picking sack. "When papá and mamá first came to the United States, we all used to work. Now not so many children pick the crops. Some of these men live here, but some left their families in Mexico. When the harvests are finished, they will go back home."

Peter's dad walked over from the stacked bins. "How did these two do, Rosalía?"

"They will be very good pickers, Mr. Lewis. They are careful, and they work hard."

"Spoken like a true diplomat." Peter grinned at Rosalía. "She's not telling you that she picked at least two sacks to my one."

The three said good-bye. At the ranch house, Megan asked Rosalía when the school bus came by.

"At 4:30," she said. "See you at the bus stop."

In the kitchen, Aunt Gladys had just put a pan of cornbread into the oven. Peter lifted the lid from a pot of soup.

"Mmmm! Cabbage patch? I love it."

"That's what it is." Aunt Gladys straightened and smiled at the grubby pair. "My, you certainly look like apple pickers! You have time to shower while the cornbread bakes."

"You go first, Megan. I've got to feed Jiggs."

Megan stopped by her room to grab clean clothes before heading for the shower. From the window, she saw her stepfather and Carlos Salinas talking together. Luis was with them.

"Lord, I know You want us to help others whether or not they thank us," she grumbled. "But I sure don't understand what makes that guy tick."

By the time Megan had dressed and dried her hair, Peter was ready too. Aunt Gladys dished them bowls of the cabbage patch soup. "You two have a long evening ahead of you. Better eat hearty."

Peter reached for the plate of cornbread and passed it to Megan. "What a day!" he said. "I never realized the work that goes into getting the apples picked and to market."

Aunt Gladys sat down at the table with them. Her normally cheerful face showed a hint of worry. "Yes. Martin's accident couldn't have happened at a worse time."

"How was Uncle Martin this afternoon?" Megan asked.

"He's feeling better," Aunt Gladys answered. "Of course, he's frustrated that he can't work. But he's thankful you're here to help."

Megan spooned up her last bit of soup and looked at the kitchen clock. "It's 4:15," she cried. "We'll miss the bus!" She hopped up and carried her dishes to the dishwasher.

Aunt Gladys gave them each a hug and hurried them out the door. "I'll be praying for you."

Peter and Megan ran down the hill to the Salinas home and knocked. Alicia opened the door.

"Luis and Rosalía? They just left to catch the school bus." Megan thanked her and hurried after Peter toward the main road. A cold, scared feeling settled in her insides. If they missed the bus, they'd have to get someone to take them to town. And they'd have to walk into a strange school alone.

But the Salinas twins were waiting at the stop, and just as Megan and Peter reached it, the bus pulled up. Several other teenagers—all Hispanic—were already on the bus. Megan felt their curious stares as she and Peter made their way to a seat. Luis slid in beside another boy and ignored them, but Rosalía plopped down in front of them and turned around with a bright smile. She wore

77

her nicest clothes and her hair curled shiny and fluffy against her shoulders.

"This is the best part of the day!" she exclaimed. "You'll like night school. It's not boring like day school."

A little later they followed a stream of students into the building. "There's the office," Rosalía said. "That's where you register." She waved and disappeared down a hall.

Megan told one of the secretaries who they were. She handed her the withdrawal forms their own school had sent with them. The forms listed their grades up to now.

"Oh, yes. Mrs. Wirth called to tell us to expect you." The secretary came around the counter. "Follow me. I'll get one of the counselors to set up a schedule for you."

Megan sat with Peter in uncomfortable molded plastic chairs while the counselor checked the classes they had been taking at home. "You're enrolling for only two or three weeks?"

Megan nodded yes. The counselor pushed her glasses back up onto her hair. "Well, from the looks of your grades, you shouldn't have any trouble."

A bell rang as the counselor finished making out their schedules. "I'll put you both in the same classes," she said. "That will be easier all around."

She handed each of them a schedule. "Your first class is World History with Miss Vivanco. I'll show you where to go." She led them down a hall empty of students.

The first day at a new school and we're late to our first class, Megan thought, the blood pounding loudly in her ears.

The counselor opened a classroom door, and two dozen faces turned from the petite, dark-haired teacher to stare at them. Megan and Peter followed the counselor to the teacher's desk. Someone smiled and lifted a hand as they passed. Rosalía! And Luis sat a couple of rows away.

"Welcome," Miss Vivanco said to them. She glanced quickly at the admittance slip the counselor handed her and turned to the class. "Peter Lewis and Megan Parnell will be joining us for a few weeks. They are from Madrona Bay, in western Washington." She began to count out papers for the first person in each row to pass back. "We're having a quiz first thing," she told Peter and Megan. "You may not have covered the same material but do your best. There are a couple of empty seats back there behind Sam." She pointed to the seats she meant.

Oh, great! Late to class and we're hit with a test we haven't studied for, Megan thought. She clutched her notebook tighter as she followed Peter down the aisle. The boy Miss Vivanco called Sam sat like a small mountain in the last occupied seat, his pudgy face and short fat neck sloping into rounded shoulders and an overgrown body. One thick leg extended into the aisle. As Peter approached, Megan saw Sam's broad, heavy lips twist in a sneer; his little eyes almost disappeared into folds of fat. Too late for Peter to avoid it, Sam's foot flopped sideways, catching him at the ankle and sending him stumbling into the desk across the aisle.

Megan gasped. The girl who sat there grabbed for her pen and books. She looked annoyed. "Grow up, you guys!" she hissed.

Megan scowled at Sam, who smirked as Peter apologized and slid with burning face into the seat behind the girl, leaving the one behind Sam for Megan. Right now, Megan knew, Peter would give anything to be back home in Madrona Bay.

So would she.

Malicious Mischief

Megan chewed on her pencil, trying to think of the name of the president who'd led America out of the Great Depression. Was it Roosevelt ... Theodore Roosevelt? No, not Theodore. Frank? Franklin! She wrote *Franklin D. Roosevelt* after the last question on her paper.

The hulking boy ahead of her exhaled noisily and slammed himself against the back of his seat, scooting it into Megan's desk. Her pencil jolted a dark scribble up the page, right through her answers.

"Sam!" Miss Vivanco admonished.

"This is hard, Teach!" the big oaf whined.

"We've gone over all of this in class, Sam." The teacher looked at her watch. "Time's up," she said to the students. "Pass your papers forward, please."

She asked a student to get textbooks for Peter and Megan. The class went over the quiz, then Miss Vivanco explained the assignment for the next day. "In the remaining 15 minutes, you may study with partners or alone," she said.

The classroom rumbled with clatter and scraping as students moved their chairs to sit beside someone else. Rosalía moved her chair next to Peter's and beckoned to Megan to scoot hers over. Megan picked up her book, then glanced at Sam. Nobody had offered to sit beside him, and he obviously could use help with history. Obnoxious as he seemed, perhaps she should try to befriend him—though she suspected in so doing she might commit social suicide.

She tapped Sam's shoulder, and when the boy turned, she held out her book in an invitation to be partners. Sam stared at her, surprise and uncertainty in his face. Then he arranged his features in a couldn't-careless look.

"Naw," he said, "I already know that stuff." He stretched out his legs and slouched down with his neck on the back of his chair, head almost resting on Megan's desk. He propped his book on his chest and stared at the ceiling.

I tried, Megan thought, wondering why someone so lazy would bother to come to night school. She pulled her desk back. She'd join Rosalía and Peter. Then, seeing them already deep in discussion, she decided against it and opened the textbook—the same book her class at Madrona High used. She'd studied the chapter a couple of weeks ago so she only pretended to read, unable to keep her mind on history.

She didn't know about Peter, but she'd felt ... well, sort of *noble*, sacrificing time with her friends and activities in Madrona Bay to come help Uncle Martin. Shouldn't things be going along a little more smoothly than they had been going so far?

She made a disgusted face at the top of the straw-colored head still resting on the seat back in front of her. Sam's ears moved slightly in a jerky rhythm, as if he was chewing gum. Suddenly he lurched upright and appeared to hunch over his book. Well, she thought. Guess he's changed his mind about studying.

Her mind wandered to the project she was supposed to do for the history and English teachers in Madrona Bay. "Write a report about some part of the fruit-growing industry," they'd said. She already had her topic, the migrant workers. Attending these night classes would give her more insight. She'd just ask lots of questions and keep her eyes open.

"Ouch!" All faces turned at Rosalía's startled exclamation. Rosalía rubbed her cheek and glared at Sam. Across the room, Luis swiveled toward his sister. Then he too glared at Sam.

"Why ya lookin' at me?" Sam protested in an injured voice. "I didn't do nothin'." He jerked his thumb toward Peter. "Why don't ya blame him?" He leaned out of his seat and twisted to look under Peter's desk. "See? Spit wads."

Sure enough, several wads of paper lay scattered beneath the desk. Miss Vivanco clicked across the floor to stand between them.

"The Hulk threw those, Miss Vivanco," said the girl in front of Peter. "I saw him."

"The people in this class are here because they want to get an education, Sam."

"Why does everybody always blame me?"

The bell cut his complaint short. Megan gathered her belongings and slipped out of the room. She saw Luis and the boy he'd studied with saunter down the hall. The other boy was latino too, with a hard look about his eyes.

Peter and Rosalía caught up. "Rosalía's going to show us where our English class is," Peter said. "She has a different class." He turned to their friend. "I'm sorry about the spit wad. Really, I didn't throw it."

"I know." She smiled up at him. "It was the Hulk. He's mean. Especially to the mexicanos." She pronounced the x like h, "mehicanos."

"Why is he in night school if he doesn't want to learn?" Peter asked.

"Someone said he has to take care of his little brothers during the day because his mother left them," Rosalía said. "I feel sorry for the little brothers."

At break time, Megan and Peter bought snacks and soda from vending machines and wandered outside into the school courtyard. In the cool dusk, kids chatted with their own groups of friends, paying very little attention to the newcomers. Funny, Megan thought. I never really understood how lonesome it is to be new in school. But some of the migrant kids have to do this several times a year. At least Peter's here, and we have Rosalía.

Rosalía stopped with her can of soda. "May I join you?"

"Sure. Where's Luis?" Peter asked.

"Over there," Rosalía made a face as she gestured toward the far side of the courtyard, "with Tomás and Eduardo."

Tomás was the boy Luis had studied with earlier.

"The Hulk—Sam—leaves those two alone. But I do not like my brother to be with them. They are ... how do you say it? Tough guys?"

The next two classes, chemistry and math, went quickly. At 9:00, Rosalía walked with them to their bus. When it let them off at Uncle Martin's long driveway, Luis had little to say, though Rosalía chattered cheerfully as they walked under the stars.

"I'm glad they don't expect us to do homework in night school," Peter sighed after the others turned in at their own house. "6:00 A.M. is going to come awfully early."

They came to the orchard, row after row of trees whose dark shadows pooled eerily on the moonlit roadway. The soft dust muffled Megan's and Peter's footsteps.

Suddenly Megan heard something scuffing through the dry grasses under the trees some distance off but coming closer. She grabbed Peter's arm. He'd heard it too. "Probably just deer looking for windfalls," he whispered.

They moved quietly ahead, then stopped in the shadows and looked back. Whatever it was had reached the drive and paused. Had it seen them? Megan's heart began to pound as a dark shape, then another, moved onto the road. Staying in the shadows, the shapes headed toward the highway. Just as the drive curved out of sight, two thin, scraggly-haired figures wearing bulky backpacks came full into the moonlight.

~~~~~~~~~~~~~~~~~~

At 6:00 A.M., Megan's alarm jolted her out of a sound sleep. Groggily, she pulled on her picking clothes. She

85

brushed her teeth and washed her face, then, smelling coffee, followed her nose to the kitchen.

"May I have a cup of that coffee, Aunt Gladys? My eyes don't want to stay open!"

"Poor girl! Why don't you go back to bed for an hour?"

"I'd love to, but I came to pick apples, and that's what I'm going to do," she said. "Isn't Peter up?"

"I'm here." Peter dragged into the kitchen, looking as tired as she felt. They'd told Peter's dad and Aunt Gladys about the nocturnal visitors in the orchard as soon as they got home last night. Darren had said he'd take a look around first thing in the morning. That's what he was doing now, Megan supposed.

Aunt Gladys told them to sit down at the table and set plates of steaming hotcakes and bacon before them. "How do you like your eggs?" she asked.

"Over easy for me," Peter said.

"Me too," Megan said. "This looks great, Aunt Gladys."

A few minutes later, feeling more awake, Megan followed Peter out the back door. The sun had barely crested the hills across the valley, but the pickers had already arrived. She saw Mr. Salinas telling them where to begin.

Jiggs frolicked around the two while Peter filled a plastic bucket with water for his dog. Carrying their picking sacks and the water, they started toward Mr. Salinas to get their assignments. Megan saw her stepfather emerge from the trees some distance down the hill. Even at a distance, his expression looked grim.

"Something's wrong, Peter."

Peter followed her gesture. "Let's go meet him."

As soon as they reached him, Darren said, "Well, it appears the men you saw last night were up to no good. The irrigation pond's been drained again, and this time they smashed the pumps too."

"Then it *wasn't* rockchucks that caused the washout last spring," Megan said.

"Maybe not. Remember, Uncle Martin said he'd seen a couple of suspicious characters in the orchard before that washout too."

"But why?" Peter asked. "Why would somebody do something like that?"

"It's malicious mischief," said his father. "Maybe someone has a grudge."

"Who'd be mad at Uncle Martin?" Even as she asked it, Megan remembered the accident that Luis had said was really not accidental. Scud Sawyer had been the driver of the tractor that hurt Uncle Martin. But why should he have a grudge? Besides, she felt certain neither of the men they'd seen last night was Scud Sawyer.

She and Peter began the morning's picking close to where they'd found the swarming bees last spring. Megan heard Peter telling the bee story to Rosalía, who was picking in an adjacent tree, but the vandalism to the pond and pumps occupied her thoughts. Why now? The water wasn't needed for irrigation at this time of year, and the damage could certainly be repaired long before need for the sprinklers next spring.

The hours blurred into repetition: Climb the ladder, fill the bag, climb down the ladder, empty the bag, over and over. Backs and shoulders grew sore, the still air stifling. Around 11:00, the four stopped to eat their sandwiches, with Luis still sulkily silent. Then they went back to work.

Megan had just wrestled her ladder to another tree and climbed it when a small breeze rustled through the leaves. She lifted her face to its cooling breath, then wrinkled her nose. She'd caught a whiff of smoke. The smell grew stronger. She climbed down her ladder and stooped to look beneath the foliage, up and down the rows of tree trunks, but saw nothing. "I smell smoke, Peter," she called up to him.

She watched him stop picking and sniff. "Me too. Maybe someone's burning brush."

"Maybe." After what had happened last night, she felt uneasy. "I'll be right back." She patted Jiggs, then walked to the wire fence.

She looked downhill toward where the empty pond lay, but saw only last spring's grasses, now tinder-dry and bleached by the sun. In the opposite direction, tan hillsides rose to meet a clear blue sky except that some distance up the hillside, little plumes of smoke eddied in the breeze and gathered into a filmy swirl against the sky. At the base of the smoke, orange tongues of flame licked out into the dry grass and weeds. A strengthening wind began to push the flames down the hill, toward them and Uncle Martin's orchard.

Panic like a big hand slammed her in the chest and left her voiceless, but only for a moment. She gulped a deep breath and screamed, "Fire! Help!" A gust whipped cinders and burning twigs into the air and dropped them ahead of the fire. Curls of smoke puffed up in a dozen new spots. "Fire!" she screamed again. "It's coming this way!"

In a flash, Luis was beside her. "Wildfire," he yelled in Spanish. Shouts erupted from throughout the orchard.

"Rosalía, Peter, Megan—run!" Luis ordered. "Go to the ranch house! Bring shovels and gunny sacks."

He climbed through the barbed wire fence and headed toward the fire, calling to other pickers to follow. They started to stamp out the small spot fires.

Megan whirled and dashed after Peter and Rosalía. They passed Carlos and other pickers rushing toward the fire. Jiggs barked. She noticed the bucket of water next to the tree where he was tied. It was such a little bit. If only the pond and the pumps hadn't been vandalized. They could have used the pond water to fight the flames.

Peter hurriedly untied Jiggs and raced with him to catch up with the girls. Aunt Gladys had seen the smoke and come running. "There's a fire," Megan gasped. "We need shovels and burlap bags."

"In the shed," Aunt Gladys said, pointing to a building below the house. "I'll find some old rugs. And I'll call the fire department."

Shovels and pitchforks hung on the shed's wall. Peter found old burlap bags in a pile in a corner, and they took those too. Megan snatched up a couple of buckets. "Let's soak the sacks first," she said, knowing that Luis wanted them for beating out the flames. "They won't burn if they're wet."

She ran to the faucet beside the house and turned it on full force. As the buckets filled, she shoved the sacks down into the water. When all were soaked, Megan stuffed as many as would fit back into her two buckets to carry. Rosalía carried the rest, not worrying that she too got soaked. Peter struggled toward the orchard with a load of unwieldy tools. By now, the column of smoke had become a fast-spreading cloud.

The tractor roared down the hill, Darren hanging on behind Scud Sawyer. He leaped off and swung the buckets and the wet bags onto the tractor. Scud climbed down. "Pile the tools across the tines of the forklift," Darren shouted. Peter dropped them at Scud's feet and dashed to the shed to get those he'd not been able to carry. He brought some rope as well. He helped Scud use it to lash the tools in place.

Aunt Gladys ran out of the house with an armload of old bathroom and scatter rugs. "The firemen are on their way. I'll stay here and show them where to go."

Darren gave her a quick hug and took the rugs. "Thanks, these will help. I don't know if the fire trucks can get close enough, but tell them to follow me up the perimeter road. I've already cut the fence."

He jumped into the seat of the tractor, leaving Scud to come on foot, and roared back up the hill to the upper edge of the orchard. The cloud of smoke grew larger.

Aunt Gladys tried to smile, but Megan saw her mouth tremble. What if the fire reached the orchard? What if it reached the ranch buildings? What would the Wirths do then?

Trouble with the Hulk

By the time Megan, Peter, and Rosalía had raced back through the orchard, the tractor was already at the hillside. Luis and the other pickers, forced to retreat in front of the advancing fire, rushed to grab shovels or wet burlap bags.

Smoke stung Megan's eyes and burned her throat. Her heart pounded against her breastbone as if it would burst. "Help us, Lord," she gasped. Snatching up one of the bags, she ran to join the line of workers beating out the flames. Others rushed back and forth on the hill below them, putting out small fires started by the wind-blown embers.

Megan felt the ground's heat through the soles of her shoes. Sparks flew through the choking smoke and stung her bare arms.

"Hold still," someone next to her ordered as a thump on her upper back knocked her off balance. She whirled, ready to fight, then smelled burned hair and realized it was her own. Anger turned to gratitude.

"Luis, is that you?" His face was so black she had to look twice. "Thanks. I owe you." She twisted her singed hair back under her hat, surprised and touched by the concern she'd seen in Luis' dark eyes, and picked up her smoldering burlap bag.

Shouts announced the arrival of firefighters from town. With relief, Megan and the other pickers fell back to leave the front line to the professionals. Soon all that remained of the fire was a large patch of blackened hillside and a few curls of smoke.

Darren Lewis appeared, soot-smeared and exhausted. "Thanks, you guys. If you hadn't been such quick thinkers, we might not have stopped that fire."

"I wonder how it started," Peter mused.

"I'd like to know that too," Darren answered. "Why don't you kids quit for the afternoon? You've earned a rest."

Megan looked at her watch. By the time she scrubbed all this dirt and soot off, it would almost be time for school. But first, she needed a drink of water— at least a gallon—to cool her parched and smoke-clogged throat.

She and Peter and the twins found Aunt Gladys with Mrs. Salinas and the younger children on the ranch house lawn setting up a table with sandwiches and big pitchers of cold drinks for those who'd fought the fire. Jiggs romped with Teodoro.

Aunt Gladys hugged each of them, ignoring the dirt and soot. "Thank you, thank you *all* for what you did. And thank God for helping you!"

Later, after Megan had lathered away the soot and the smell of smoke, she stood before the bathroom mirror, assessing the damage to her hair. Not too bad, thanks to Luis—one or two locks a little shorter than the others and some frizzed ends. She'd ask Aunt Gladys to trim them for her as soon as the excitement died down.

As she dressed for school, she thought of all that had gone wrong for the Wirths this year. First the damaged reservoir last spring. Then Uncle Martin's accident and the new damage to the reservoir. Now the fire. It all seemed increasingly less like coincidence.

"I'm afraid Martin will hear about the fire on the news," Aunt Gladys said when all the firefighters had left. Since she wanted to reassure him in person that all was well at the ranch, she offered to drive Megan, Peter, and the Salinas twins to school on her way to the hospital.

The bell for first class had already rung when they entered the building. Rosalía hurried on, but Peter had to stop at his locker for his books. Megan paused to wait for him. Luis waited beside her.

Almost shyly, Luis touched the tresses that brushed her shoulders, then he snatched his hand away. "I am glad the fire did not hurt your pretty hair." His gentle gesture brought a flush to her cheeks and an answering touch of color burned on his high cheekbones, as if he felt he'd been too bold.

Luis could be a pain at times, but he'd saved her from serious injury. And his quick thinking in sending them for help while he attacked the spot fires may well have saved the ranch from disaster.

"I'm glad you were there, Luis." She smiled at him. His cheeks reddened, and he looked down at the floor.

"Okay, I'm ready." Peter banged his locker door shut. "Let's go."

They sprinted past the rest of the lockers, rounded the hall corner, and skidded to a stop. Like a bad dream,

Sam the Hulk loomed in front of them, a sneer twisting his thick lips. His little eyes shot daggers at Megan, then Luis. Obviously he'd been lurking and listening.

Luis had to tilt his head back to meet the Hulk's eyes. Megan saw a muscle twitch in his jaw, but he kept his voice steady. "Let us pass, please."

"What's your hurry?" Football-sized fists came out of Sam's pockets. "You beaners usually got all the time in the world. You got time to talk to me."

Luis tried to step around Sam, but Sam, lurching sideways to block his way, trapped Luis against the concrete block wall. Megan gasped. "We're late for class, Sam," she said. "Let us by." The Hulk glanced contemptuously at her but didn't answer. With shock, she realized he resented her being with Luis. Was that what all this was about?

"When I'm through with you, you'll stay away from the white girls." A massive fist whistled toward Luis' jaw. Luis ducked.

The fist crashed into the concrete wall. The bully yelped and sucked at his scraped knuckles, his little eyes glaring red and hot at Luis. He lumbered forward with his fists raised. Luis backed toward the corner.

"Stop it, Sam!" Peter demanded, but the Hulk ignored him.

As Luis backed around the corner, Sam swung again. Luis dodged. "Ooomph!" Sam's fist connected with something soft but solid. Megan watched the look of triumph on Sam's face melt into one of shocked horror. She reacted in horror herself as she saw tall Principal Deming grab his stomach with both hands, double over, and drop to his knees. Pain twisted his face; he gasped for breath.

"Mr. Deming!" Megan cried, dashing to him. "Mr. Deming, are you hurt?"

Mr. Deming raised his head, speechless.

Without a word, Sam turned, ran down the hall, and out the door.

Mr. Deming, tie askew and strands of hair falling over his balding forehead, struggled to his feet. Luis glanced around with a look of desperation but stood his ground.

The principal's words came out in squeaky gasps. "What was that all about? Will somebody please explain."

Luis set his jaw and said nothing.

"We weren't doing anything, Mr. Deming," Peter said. "The Hulk just picked a fight."

Megan saw that Luis wasn't going to defend himself, so she spoke up. "He called Luis a beaner and said he'd teach him to stay away from white girls."

"Suppose ... you three come talk to me after ... I get my wind back. My secretary will call you ... out of class." Still hunched over, Mr. Deming fumbled a piece of paper from his jacket pocket and scribbled his signature on it. With a shaking hand, Megan took the admit slip. In class, she gave it to Miss Vivanco, then slid into her seat.

Rosalía passed a note to her. "Why were you late?"

"Tell you later," Megan mouthed.

Fifteen minutes later, the secretary's voice came over the intercom. "Peter Lewis, Megan Parnell, and Luis Salinas, report to the office."

To their surprise, Sam slouched in an outer office chair. He didn't look up as they passed.

Mr. Deming's tie was again in place, his hair neatly combed. "Sit down, please. One of the counselors happened to be outside and brought Sam back in. I've talked to him. Now I'd like to hear from you three."

Peter repeated what they'd already told him. Mr. Deming looked at Luis. "You didn't insult Sam?"

"No," Luis said, looking surprised. "I only asked him to let us pass."

"You're sure you're not leaving anything out?" he asked each in turn.

"Megan and I believe in telling the truth, Mr. Deming," Peter said. "We've told you exactly what happened."

"All right. Sam will be suspended for a week. Maybe by then he'll have cooled off."

As the three returned to class, Miss Vivanco was giving an assignment for the next week: individual reports on the culture, history, or industries of the people in the Yakima valley.

Megan remembered the reports they were supposed to do for class at Madrona High. When Miss Vivanco asked if there were any questions, she raised her hand.

"Yes, Megan?"

"Miss Vivanco," she began, "we have to take reports back to our old school." Across the aisle, Peter's face lit up as he realized her idea. "Could we use the same report for your class?"

"What are your topics?"

"I want to find out more about migrant workers and their contribution to our economy," Megan told her.

"I wanted to write about the apple industry," Peter said. "We're picking apples for our uncle, and I'd like to know more."

"Yes," said Miss Vivanco. "Making your reports do double duty would be fine, but I'll expect you both to do a top-notch job."

"Thanks, Miss Vivanco."

At break time, Luis disappeared with Tomás and Eduardo. Peter, Megan, and Rosalía took their snacks outdoors and sat together on a cement bench that circled a big cottonwood tree. When they told Rosalía what had happened with the Hulk, Megan saw a shadow cross Rosalía's face. She turned to follow Rosalía's gaze to a far corner where Luis and his two friends lounged against the chainlink fence.

"Are you worried that Luis might bring those two guys into the fight, Rosalía?"

"Oh ... no," Rosalía said. "Well, maybe. I'm worried about what papá will say. He does not want us to get into trouble."

"Parents never want their kids to get in trouble," Megan pointed out. "But it wasn't Luis' fault."

"Some people say Tomás and Eduardo are part of a gang. I do not think so, but they run with people who are. So I am afraid for Luis, but papá is worried for a different reason."

"Why is he worried?" Peter asked.

Rosalía looked around to be sure no one was near enough to overhear. Her face showed her struggle. "You promise not to tell?"

"We promise," Megan said.

Rosalía glanced around again and lowered her voice. Peter and Megan leaned close to hear above the noise in the courtyard. "It happened a long time ago, when papá and mamá first came from Mexico. Luis and I were just babies.

"We followed the crops. When winter came, the money ran out. Mamá says we cried because we were hungry. That made papá cry too. He walked to town and didn't come back for a couple of days. Later, mamá told us what happened that night."

Tears welled in Rosalía's eyes. She took a deep breath. "My papá took some rice and milk from a grocery store without paying for it. A police officer arrested him and put him in jail."

"Oh," Megan said. "That's sad. But anyone would understand why he did it. And it was a long time ago. Why should it bother him now?"

"Because in 1986, the government passed the Immigration Reform Act, making it harder for people to stay in this country illegally. But those, like my family, who could prove they had been here before a certain date could apply for amnesty. Then they could become permanent residents, even citizens."

Megan puzzled over this. "You mean your folks were here illegally?"

"Yes. People have always come over the border from Mexico to work here. Many are desperate and come without official permission. But now the law punishes employers who hire illegal workers and makes it harder for those workers to stay here."

"Didn't your father apply for this amnesty?" she asked.

"No," Rosalía said, "mamá did, but papá was afraid if the officials found out about his arrest, they would send us back to Mexico. So he got some false documents, and nobody knows we are illegal aliens. Well, mamá is legal, and so are the younger children. They were born here so they are citizens, but they cannot stay without papá to take care of them."

"So that's why your father doesn't want any trouble," Peter said. "He's afraid someone will find out his secret."

"It's more than just about our family," Rosalía almost whispered.

The meaning of what she'd said a few minutes earlier about the law punishing employers suddenly hit Megan. "You mean Uncle Martin could get in trouble too?"

Rosalía's head drooped, and she nodded. "I ... I guess he could."

"That's not fair!" Megan exclaimed. "Uncle Martin doesn't even know about this, does he?"

"No." Rosalía looked up, dark eyes frightened. "Oh, why did I tell you? I just made everything worse."

"We promised not to tell," Megan said, "and we won't."

What a mess, she thought as the three sat in a dejected huddle. Uncle Martin could be fined or even go to jail when he'd only meant to help the Salinas family. That one mistake could wind up shattering the dreams of the whole family, and it seemed they could do nothing. No, there was *something* they could do. Megan caught Rosalía's hand. "God knows all about this," she told her friend. "He'll show us an answer if we ask Him."

The bell shrilled, and they got up. A stealthy movement behind the big cottonwood caught Megan's attention. She glimpsed Sam the Hulk sliding away into the stream of kids entering the building.

"Was he spying?" Rosalía asked.

"The big jerk!" Megan scowled after him, then turned to Rosalía. "Don't worry—even if he was, I'm sure it was too noisy out here for him to hear what we said."

When school let out that evening, Megan, Peter, and the Salinas twins waited to board their bus. Sam walked by lugging his books for assignments to be done while he was suspended.

He stepped close. "Think you're pretty smart, don't ya?" he sneered at Luis. "You just wait. I'll get even." He glared at each in turn. "I'll get even with all of ya."

By the time Megan, Peter, Luis, and Rosalía got off the bus, the day's excitement had caught up with them. Megan and Peter said good-bye and dragged themselves up the hill to the ranch house. They said good night to Peter's dad and Aunt Gladys, both of whom also looked exhausted, and tumbled into their beds without mentioning the confrontation with the Hulk. Megan fell asleep thanking God for His protection that day and reminding Him that the Salinas family needed help.

She awoke the next morning, Saturday, to the sound of the straddle buggy growling up the driveway. She shrugged into her robe and staggered to the window, rubbing the sleep out of her eyes. By the position of the sun she knew she'd overslept. She saw Carlos Salinas come out of the orchard. By way of hand signals he guided the truck into place over a long stack of filled bins. The hydraulic lift whooshed as it moved the frame into place beneath the stack, then eased it off the ground.

Scud Sawyer drove the forklift out of the orchard with a couple of full bins. He deposited them atop the beginnings of a new load for the straddle buggy, which lumbered away down the hill. Scud whipped the tractor around to a huge stack of empty bins. He picked up several on the forklift, then whirled it around again and sped down the hill. He disappeared into the lower part of the orchard, a cloud of dust boiling up behind him.

She frowned, wondering what his hurry was.

At breakfast, Aunt Gladys seemed preoccupied—not her usual cheerful self. Megan swallowed the last of her milk and hopped up. "Give me your dishes, Peter. I'll put them in the dishwasher with mine. Are you ready to go?"

"As ready as I'm going to get. Thanks for breakfast, Aunt Gladys." Peter lifted the picking sacks from their hook in the back entry and snapped the leash to Jiggs' collar. "Come on, fella."

"Poor dog! Can't he be untied?" Megan asked.

"I guess so." Peter took the leash off again. "He knows to stay with us now."

Jiggs trotted ahead of them across the back lawn. Passing the corner of the house, they saw Luis and Rosalía trudging up the hill with their picking sacks. Just as Rosalía raised her arm in greeting, the tractor barreled out from between the trees.

The forklift's prongs swung toward the twins. Scud Sawyer shouted, but he didn't stop. Dust from the tractor hid them from Megan's view, and she gasped.

As the dust settled, Megan let out her breath. Luis and Rosalía were all right!

"He called us a name for being in his way," Rosalía fumed as they came within earshot. She was still trembling. "We weren't in his way! He was driving too fast."

The four headed toward the rows where the pickers worked. The tractor roared down the hill with another load of empty bins, forcing them to step off the road.

Carlos Salinas met them at the edge of the orchard. "I saw," he said to the twins, gazing after the tractor through narrowed eyes. "Sawyer ... he one mean hombre!"

"He's an accident waiting to happen," Peter said. "Where's my dad, Mr. Salinas?"

"He say somebody put something in ranch truck's gas tank. He went to Sunnyside to order new engine. That is why Sawyer drive fast."

Sunnyside was at least an hour's drive away. Carlos obviously felt Scud thought he could get away with recklessness when the boss wasn't there. But the suggestion of sabotage was what caught Megan's attention. What had been put in the gas tank? Who was responsible and why?

Peter gave voice to her thoughts. "There's a lot of funny stuff going on around here. We'd all better keep our eyes open."

Mr. Salinas nodded somberly. He gave them their picking tickets and told them where to start work. They found their trees and set up their ladders. Megan tore the stub off one of her tickets and began to tie the larger part on the same bin Rosalía and Luis had fastened theirs to.

Luis put out his hand to stop her. "You pick much better than you did at first," he said and smiled. "No more excuses. Put your ticket on a bin of your own. We want you and Peter to keep what you earn from now on."

Megan grinned. He had seen through her earlier subterfuge. "Well, if that's what you want ..."

The time passed quickly. Jiggs explored among the trees for a while, then curled up to nap near them. Peter and Megan filled their bin and started on another.

"I'm thirsty," said Rosalía.

"Me too," Peter answered. "Let's get a drink of water." The four, followed by Jiggs, walked through the trees. They were enjoying the cool water when they heard the sound of the forklift approaching.

"Stay out of his way, everybody!" Peter warned.

Everyone laughed. Ducking between the trees, they returned to their own aisle. Scud Sawyer had lifted a bin on the tines of the forklift. Just as a couple of pickers started to cross in front of him, he jabbed the accelerator and then braked so hard the tractor nearly stood on its nose. The pickers jumped to get out of his way. Apples bounced from the bin.

"Watch where you're going, ya good-fer-nothin' tacos," Scud shouted.

Rosalía gasped. "He yelled at papá!"

When the men turned, Megan saw the picking foreman silently watching Sawyer from the shadows of a tree. Recognizing Mr. Salinas, Jiggs galloped over to greet him.

The ill-tempered driver headed the tractor toward the bin Peter and Megan had filled. He slid the tines under it, then, looking over his shoulder, raised the lift at the same time as he put the tractor into reverse. As the forklift came around, they saw clearly that Scud had not aimed dead center, and only the left tine had gone through the space beneath the bin. The other tine touched the outside of the box and looked for a moment as if it would keep it from tipping. But Scud jerked the wheel in a sharp right turn. The bin slid to the left, then rotated on the tine.

"Oh, no," Megan said.

The apples she and Peter had worked so hard to pick spilled like marbles from a giant's toybox into the dusty grass.

A string of curse words sizzled through the air. Scud lowered the tines and backed away from the nearly empty bin.

"Hey! Those were our apples!" Megan cried.

Scud Sawyer glared. "Then get busy and pick them up," he retorted. "Your fault anyway—why don't you leave that dumb mutt home where he belongs?" Open-mouthed, Megan stared. Scud backed up, lifted one of Luis' boxes instead, and drove away.

"*Our* fault!" Megan exclaimed. "How can he say that?"

"Jiggs didn't do anything," Peter fumed. He knelt down to hug his dog, who'd come running over to investigate the heap of spilled apples. Mr. Salinas came over too.

"Won't these be all bruised now, Mr. Salinas?" Megan asked.

"Some bruised, yes," he answered. "Pick up anyway. Okay for juice."

"We'll help you," offered Rosalía, filling her sack with apples from the ground. Mr. Salinas and a couple of pickers who had seen what happened pitched in to help. By the time Scud Sawyer returned with the tractor, all the apples were back in the bin. But they were dusty and marred with dents that would bruise, then spoil.

At noon, the four young people carried their lunch sacks to the fence where the orchard met the dry hillside where the fire had burned. They lay in the grassy shade beneath a tree, eating and chatting. Jiggs begged for bits of sandwich until Peter parted the strands of barbed wire enough for him to get through. "Go find a rockchuck," he told the dog. Jiggs looked questioningly over his shoulder at his master then trotted off.

Megan finished her sandwich. "Aunt Gladys plans to take us to the library in town this afternoon when she goes to visit Uncle Martin," she told Rosalía and Luis. "Do you want to come along? We're going to do research for our class reports."

"We can't," Luis said.

Before she could ask why, they heard excited, high-pitched barking from the hillside. Peter whistled, then whistled again, but Jiggs didn't come.

"I'd better go see what he's found." Peter rolled to his feet and climbed through the fence.

A sudden idea made Megan leap up too. "Let's all go," she said. "Maybe we can find a clue to how that fire started yesterday."

Luis hesitated. "We should get back to work ..."

"Oh, come on," she urged. "Just a few minutes?"

He gave in. "All right, Madam Detective. Just a few minutes!"

They tramped through the crackling dry weeds and grasses, following Jiggs' bursts of frantic barking. Megan kept her eyes on the ground but saw nothing but scuffed dirt and broken weeds where the firefighters had worked. "There's Jiggs," Peter said, pointing up the hill to a rocky outcropping in the middle of the burned-over patch. "He did just what I told him to do—he's found a rockchuck."

"He's trying to follow it down the tunnel!" Rosalía said, laughing at Jiggs' wildly gyrating tail and hindquarters. Dirt flew from his excavation.

Megan walked across the black ground slowly, continuing to scan for clues. She saw nothing unusual. Behind her, Rosalía and Peter stopped to cheer Jiggs on. Luis walked parallel to her up the hill, also searching the ground. Suddenly he stooped to examine something, then raised his head and beckoned.

"What is it?" Megan asked as she approached.

He pointed at a blackened object propped between two small rocks. It was a circular piece of glass with a band of metal around the edge. A twisted glob that had once been a plastic handle still hung from the bottom of it. Megan picked it up and rubbed at the soot. "This is it, Luis! A magnifying lens." She placed it back among the rocks. "See? It focused the sun's rays into the dry grass. When the grass got hot enough, it burst into flames."

"I know how a magnifying glass works. But why would it be here?"

"Someone could have lost it. But more likely ..."

"Someone used it to start the fire," he finished for her. "Maybe the same people who drained the irrigation pond?"

Megan thought of the two strangers they'd seen in the orchard. "You're a pretty good detective yourself,

Luis! They could have put it here the night they drained the pond. By the time the sun reached the right angle, there was no water left in the pond to fight the fire."

They showed Peter and Rosalía the ruined lens. Luis put it in his pocket. "Let's see what else we can find," he said, forgetting his eagerness to get back to work. The four fanned out, working up the hillside, then zigzagged back toward the orchard.

"Here's another one," Rosalía sang out. They hurried over to her. There, near an unburned pile of dry sticks and leaves, lay an undamaged lens. "See," she said. "It was probably propped against these stones, but it fell over, so nothing happened."

"We shouldn't touch it, in case there are finger-prints," Megan said.

"Here. Use this." Luis unknotted the bandanna he always wore around his neck and handed it to her.

Using a corner of the kerchief, she picked up the lens, wrapped the fabric around it, and handed it to Luis to carry in his pocket with the other. "We'd better give them to Darren," she said. "I think they'll prove the fire was arson."

They returned to the orchard and picked up their sacks. "Aunt Gladys said she'd be ready to take us to the library after lunch," Peter reminded Megan.

"That's right," Megan answered. "Luis, Rosalía, are you sure you can't go?"

"Rosalía can go if papá says yes," Luis told them. "I need to stay and pick."

"Where can Rosalía go?" Carlos Salinas appeared from between two trees.

Rosalía told her father about the invitation.

"You do school work at library?" Her father's mustache lifted in a smile. "That is good. Luis, you go too."

Luis looked none too happy but he answered, "Yes, papá."

"We'll pick in your bin Monday," Peter said. "That will help make up for the apples you'd have picked while we're gone."

Luis shook his head.

"Please let us," said Megan. "And besides, we're going to stop first at the hospital. A visit from all four of us would make Uncle Martin happy. And I think working on our reports with you and Rosalía would be fun."

"Okay," Luis said, a smile flickering across his brown face. "You win. I'll go."

They left the orchard together. Luis handed Megan the bandanna-wrapped magnifying glasses, and he and Rosalía headed toward their house to get ready. "See you in a little while," Megan called.

Beyond the ranch house, she and Peter saw the parked forklift and an old bicycle, which leaned against a stack of empty apple bins. As they neared the back porch, Scud Sawyer's angry voice echoed down the slope.

"Stupid, clumsy dimwit! Can't you do anything right?" His tirade continued in a string of curse words.

"Somebody's really getting bawlcd out," said Peter.

"Would he dare to talk to one of the pickers like that?"

"It's not a picker," Peter answered. "Look!"

The object of the tongue-lashing backed into the open. "Dad, I couldn't help it." Sam the Hulk hunched

109

his shoulders and shuffled his feet. He gestured toward some twine dangling from the package rack on the bicycle. "The string didn't hold. Before I could pick it up, a car hit it."

Scud Sawyer appeared, still cursing. He threw a battered lunch pail to the ground. "Thermos is broke," he shouted. "Sandwiches soaked. Move outa here before I get really mad!"

The Hulk moved. He grabbed the old bike, heaved himself astride and swung away.

"Scud is Sam's father?" Megan whispered incredulously.

"Quick, get inside. Don't let Sam know we live here!" Peter leaped for the porch steps.

"Too late." Megan hurried through the back door after him. "I'm almost sure he saw us."

"Who saw you?" Aunt Gladys looked up from the papers she was working on.

"The Hulk," said Peter.

"The boy who tried to beat up Luis?"

"The same," Peter answered. "Scud Sawyer's his dad."

"Why is the boy here?" Aunt Gladys crossed to a window overlooking the front yard and peered down the hill.

"Didn't you hear the yelling?" asked Megan. "He was bringing his dad's lunch to him, but it fell off the bike and got hit by a car. He probably rode his bike all the way from town."

"He must be tired," Aunt Gladys said. "He's stopping at the foot of the orchard to rest." She walked over to the

110

refrigerator. "I'll make Mr. Sawyer a sandwich and some coffee. Maybe that will sweeten his temper a bit."

Megan thought about offering to take the lunch to Scud Sawyer but hurried off to wash and change clothes instead. She had no desire to go near him. She felt a twinge of sympathy for his son. With Scud Sawyer for a father, no wonder Sam bullied other people.

When she came back to the kitchen, Darren Lewis had returned from town and was eating a sandwich at the table. "Sawyer's got an attitude problem," he was saying to Aunt Gladys and Peter. "The pickers don't care for him, but he's doing his work."

"He was still mad when I took a lunch to him," Aunt Gladys said, "although he did thank me. Do you think I should say something to Martin?"

"No, he'd just worry. And don't tell him about the truck either. I've found someone in town to replace the engine."

Darren finished eating and went out the door. Peter signaled to Megan to follow him. He caught up with Darren and, keeping his voice low, said, "Dad, we've found proof that someone set that fire yesterday."

Darren inspected the lenses as he listened to their story. "I think you're right," he agreed, frowning. "Thanks, guys. I'll let the fire marshal know about these."

Megan helped Aunt Gladys put the kitchen in order, then found notebooks and pens to take to the library.

Before they climbed into the minivan, Peter whistled for Jiggs. No big black dog came bounding across the yard.

"He must have stayed with the pickers," Megan said.

"I wanted to tie him in the yard while we're gone." Peter whistled again.

"He'll be all right," Aunt Gladys assured him. "Your dad will keep an eye on him."

"I guess so." With a last look around, Peter climbed into the vehicle.

When they stopped at the Salinas' driveway, Rosalía ran to meet them, her eyes sparkling. Peter opened the door and she hopped in. Luis followed.

"Thank you for inviting us, Mrs. Wirth!" Rosalía said. She held up a bunch of wild purple asters in a small pottery jar. "Teodoro picked some flowers for your husband."

As they rolled along, Megan told the twins about the Hulk's visit. "Did you see him ride by?"

"I didn't. Did you, Luis?"

"No." Luis looked somber. "Why am I not surprised to find that the Hulk is Scud Sawyer's son?"

"I think he saw us," Megan said. "If he did, he knows where we live."

"What could he do to you on the ranch?" Rosalía asked.

"Nothing, probably," she answered. But remembering the Hulk's threat at the bus stop, she found it hard to shake her uneasiness.

At the hospital, Aunt Gladys swung the minivan into the parking lot and they all got out. When they reached Uncle Martin's room they peered inside. A nurse was helping Uncle Martin onto the bed.

He looked frail in his plaid flannel robe—not like vigorous Uncle Martin at all. Pain twisted his face as he eased onto the pillows. Megan hesitated at the door, wondering as always when she visited someone in the hospital what she should say.

Aunt Gladys didn't seem bothered by the change in her husband. "Why, Martin, you've been walking!" she exclaimed.

He turned his head. The lines on his face deepened with his smile, changing him once more into the familiar Uncle Martin. "Here's my crew!" he told the nurse. "These are the guys who are picking my apples while you people pamper me."

The nurse said a friendly hello. She cranked up the head of the bed, then patted Uncle Martin's shoulder. "Better?"

"See what I mean?" Uncle Martin teased. "They spoil me."

He beckoned them to come in. Rosalía placed the jar of asters on his bedside table and he smiled again. "Beautiful. Thank you, Rosalía. Peter, Megan, I know you were here before, but I was too sick to pay much attention. What do you think of the orchard industry now?"

"It's hard work," Peter said. "But I like it."

"Luis and Rosalía are much faster pickers than we are," Megan told him. "But we're improving."

Uncle Martin directed his gaze at Luis. "And how is school, young man?"

Luis squirmed. "Okay. We are going to the city library today to work on our school reports."

"I'm glad to hear that," Uncle Martin told him. "I know your father tells you this all the time, but your school work is very important."

They stood around the bed for a while, telling Uncle Martin funny little happenings from the orchard, being careful to say nothing about Scud Sawyer or Sam. Then Aunt Gladys kissed him and promised to come back after she took the kids to the library.

"Where shall we start?" Rosalía asked as they entered the library.

"Why don't we ask the reference librarian for help?" Megan suggested.

They did and were soon seated at a long table with books and magazines piled around them. The reference librarian had suggested that Megan look in the periodical index for recent articles about migrant workers. Some were still on the magazine racks; some the librarian called up from the storage area.

She was deep in a *National Geographic* article when Peter nudged her. "It's 4:00. Aunt Gladys will be here soon."

"Oh, no," she groaned, gesturing at magazines she'd not even opened yet. "We can't check anything out without a library card."

"They have a copy machine here," he said. "I'm going to copy some information so I can read it later."

"Good idea. I'll do that too." She checked her purse for change.

Quickly she leafed through the remaining magazines, choosing an article about the amnesty law that Rosalía had mentioned and a couple of others. She photocopied them and joined the other three who were waiting outside.

In a few minutes, Aunt Gladys drove up. On the way home, she asked each of them what they were writing about, and they told her. "And what about you, Luis?" she asked.

"I'm writing about the business of running an orchard," he answered. "Someday I'm going to have my own ranch."

Megan looked at him with surprise. She'd known what he was writing about, of course, but not that he wanted orchards of his own. Luis looked a little embarrassed now that he had spoken his dream aloud.

"That's wonderful," said Aunt Gladys. "If you are really serious, Martin will be glad to teach you all he can. Of course, times are changing." Her brow furrowed, and she sighed. "More and more, farming of any kind is *big* business. You'll certainly need to have a college education."

Megan noticed the sigh. How could Luis ever go to college, poor as his family was? And even if he could go to college, owning an orchard took lots of money. *Lots* of money, like the big company that wanted to buy Uncle Martin's ranch. She pondered that thought. Offers of money hadn't persuaded Uncle Martin to sell. Could it be that the company was using its money in other ways to get what it wanted? Like hiring somebody to sabotage the reservoir, or to start the fire, or to damage machinery? Darren had told them that someone had poured sugar in the ranch truck's gas tank to ruin the engine. That certainly had been no accident.

They dropped off the twins and drove on to the ranch house. All was quiet. Peter got out and whistled for Jiggs. No big black dog appeared. "Maybe he's with Dad in the orchard." Peter dropped his notebook and papers on the back step. "I'm going to check."

"Wait. I'll put our things inside and come with you." Megan went inside and came back out to hurry with Peter to the lower edge of the orchard. Most of the remaining apple bins had been taken to the lower orchards. The tractor was gone too.

They saw Carlos Salinas with some pickers who were finishing the last few trees. "Buenas tardes," he called.

"Buenas tardes," Peter answered. He peered down the aisle between the trees. "Do you know where my dog is, Mr. Salinas?"

"Jiggs? No. I not see him."

"Where's my dad?"

Carlos pointed down the hill. "In other orchard. But he not have Jiggs."

Peter walked over to a picker in a nearby tree. Megan followed. "Have you seen my dog?"

The man looked down, and spread his hands in an "I don't understand" gesture.

"My dog," said Peter. He held his hand about the height of Jiggs' head from the ground and gave a couple of woofs. Understanding lit the man's dark eyes. "Ah ..." he smiled. "Perro." Then he shook his head in apology.

"Maybe he's digging for rockchucks," Megan suggested.

"I don't think he'd wander off by himself," Peter said bleakly.

"Let's look, anyway."

They climbed through the fence at the edge of the orchard. They checked at the sprinkler pond, repaired and filled again with water, then started upward.

Dry, prickly weeds caught their pant legs and crunched underfoot as they shouted and whistled. Ground squirrels whisked into their holes. A fat rockchuck stood up to peer at them, making a long shadow across the dusty ground. Then he too disappeared.

They crossed the scorched ground where the fire had burned and finally, out of breath, they reached the crest of the hill. They flopped down on the big rocks where they'd rested in their explorations last spring. The orchards below lay like plush green rugs against the tan countryside. Behind and to either side, hills dipped to gullies, shadowy in the lowering light.

"It will be night soon," Megan said. "There's just too much country out here to search on foot. Maybe if we could go on horseback ..."

Peter stared at her. She saw the worry in his eyes and could almost feel the coldness from that empty place in his middle spreading throughout his body.

She turned away, scanning once more the vastness around them. The thump of her pounding heart put words to Peter's fear. Where are you, Jiggs?

feel awful," Megan said. "If I hadn't suggested letting Jiggs run free ..."

"It's not your fault," he answered. "I should have made sure he came to the house when we did."

They started back toward the house. "Peter," she said, "maybe Jiggs wandered down to the highway. He could have followed someone ... maybe even the Hulk."

"No," Peter choked out, "not the Hulk. He wouldn't follow *him* anyplace!"

But what if Jiggs *had* followed someone to the highway? What if he'd been hit by a car? He could be lying hurt—or dead—in a ditch.

Aunt Gladys had supper ready when they walked into the kitchen. They told her and Darren about their fruitless search.

"It's too dark to see much, but we can drive along the road and look," Darren offered. "Get your jackets and some flashlights."

He drove the farm truck slowly along the highway for several miles in both directions while Megan and Peter knelt in the back, shining their lights into the ditches and along the roadside. They shouted Jiggs' name until they were hoarse.

That night, Megan lay awake a long time. They'd come to Yakima to help Uncle Martin, but they'd encountered nothing but trouble and more trouble.

"Jesus, please help!" She tried to think of a better prayer but could only repeat the same phrase over and over.

"We know that in all things God works for the good ..." The quiet words from Romans intruded into her tumbling thoughts. She whispered the rest of the verse. "God works for the good of those who love Him, who have been called according to His purpose."

God could turn Jiggs' being gone into good? Or the Hulk's bullying? Even all the strange happenings on the ranch? *In all things.* Clinging to that promise, she turned over and went to sleep.

At breakfast the next morning Darren told them, "We're going to stop at the hospital after church. We can check the animal shelter to see if anyone found Jiggs and left him there."

Peter's face brightened.

They hurried through the after-breakfast cleanup. "Everybody ready?" asked Peter's dad, thumbing through the yellow pages of the telephone directory. "The animal shelter isn't too far from the church. If we leave now, we can check there before the service."

The shelter's office was locked, but an attendant came when they pounded on the door. He led them through a room filled with wire cages. Cats slept or wailed in small cages in one part of the room. Other cages held dogs of all sizes, watching hopefully for their owners to come. But Jiggs was nowhere inside nor in the dog runs outside the building.

Megan blinked back tears as they returned to the office. "All those poor animals. Most of them will be put to sleep, won't they?"

The young man nodded. "Unfortunately, yes. We can keep them only a short while. We just don't have room for all the abandoned pets that come in." He turned to Peter. "Leave us a description of your dog, and your phone number. If somebody brings him in, we'll call you."

Peter couldn't remember the license number on Jiggs' dogtags, but he wrote the rest of the information on a piece of paper. Then the subdued group drove on to the little church the Wirths attended.

During the first part of the service, the pastor prayed for Uncle Martin and other people of the congregation who had needs. Megan added a silent prayer for Peter and his dog too.

After the service, people asked about Uncle Martin and how the harvest was coming. When the family gathered at the minivan, Aunt Gladys looked at her watch.

"It's lunchtime at the hospital now," she said. "Let me treat you all to a take-out picnic, then we can go see Martin."

At a drive-in, they bought hamburgers, french fries, and milk shakes, then they drove to the park where Peter had pulled Teodoro out of the river the previous spring. As they ate at a picnic table, they watched red and yellow leaves drifting from the trees. Some floated on the water, others crunched underfoot. Peter looked dejected and picked at his hamburger as if it were made of sawdust. Megan wondered if he was imagining Jiggs romping in those crackling leaves.

"It's beautiful here, isn't it?" Aunt Gladys said as she passed Megan the ketchup for her french fries. "But when the apples are harvested and the leaves fall, we know winter is close at hand."

Megan thought of Luis and Rosalía and their family. What would they do when the harvest ended? She asked Aunt Gladys.

"There's work in an orchard almost year-round," Aunt Gladys said. "We hope they'll stay right where they are."

Peter glanced over and caught Megan's eye. She knew he was thinking of Rosalía's secret too. What a dilemma! If they said anything, the Salinas family might suffer. If they didn't, Uncle Martin might suffer.

At the hospital, Uncle Martin's face looked rosier and he greeted them in a strong voice. "I'm raring to go," he said. "I'll be back in the orchard in three or four days."

"Great! You can use my picking sack," Peter told him.

Aunt Gladys smiled and patted her husband's hand. "No orchard for you for a while," she said. "But you can give all the advice you want."

"Speaking of advice," said Peter's dad, "I'm having a little trouble with the ranch pickup. Who would you suggest I get to work on it?"

A little trouble? Megan thought. The whole engine needed to be replaced. If only they could solve the mystery of who was causing the trouble at the orchard before Uncle Martin came home. She listened to the adults talk for a while. Then she and Peter excused themselves and slipped away to the hospital gift shop to pick out some postcards for their friends back home. They sat in the lobby to write them.

When he'd written his last postcard, Peter said to Megan, "Let's see if they're ready to go. Maybe Jiggs has found his way home by now."

They found the others just saying good-bye to Uncle Martin.

Megan checked her watch as they turned into the ranch driveway. Almost 4:00. Darren pulled up in the yard and shut off the engine. No big black dog came running.

As they went inside to change clothes, Peter told Megan, "I'm going to search that nearest ravine. The trees and brush in the bottom could have kept us from seeing him if he's there and hurt."

"I'll go with you. Let's ask Luis and Rosalía if they want to help us look."

They told Darren what they planned to do.

"Fine," said Peter's dad. "Just watch for rattlesnakes."

When they walked into the Salinas' yard, the younger children were playing beneath a tree. Teodoro ran to meet them, tugging at them to come see the miniature corrals they were building with twigs. Alicia and Isabel had tied sticks together with bits of yarn for pretend horses.

Teodoro showed them a small stick animal. "This is my dog." He wrapped his arms around Peter's leg and

123

looked up into his face. "I am sorry Jiggs is lost." Rosalía peered out the open window. "Hello, Peter, Megan!" She came running down the front steps. "Did you find ...?"

"No," Peter said. "We're going to search the gully. Do you want to come along?"

"I'll tell mamá," Rosalía said. She disappeared into the house and came out again with Luis. "We'll both help," she said.

They followed the highway until they saw the brushy mouth of the ravine above them, then followed the rocky pathway of a dry watercourse. Sturdy walking sticks they picked up along the way helped them over the rough footing and through the brush.

Keeping watch for rattlesnakes, they spread out and for an hour struggled upward, searching and calling. The gully curved below the irrigation pond and the orchard, rising to meet the top of the ridge that ran along the valley. They saw no snakes and no sign of Jiggs either.

The four regrouped on the back side of the hill Peter and Megan had searched yesterday. "The sun's almost down," Luis said.

Peter gazed out across the hills rolling off into the distance behind them. "You're right. We'd better get home." His voice broke. "He could be anywhere out there, hungry or hurt ..."

"He'll be okay, Peter." A quaver shook Megan's voice too as she patted her stepbrother's shoulder. "We'll find him."

The next morning, everyone worked in the lower orchard. Darren left early to see that all got off to a good start, but he told Aunt Gladys that he'd be back to give Peter and Megan a ride to the orchard. He hadn't returned by the time they were ready to go, so they walked. In the lower orchard, they found Rosalía and the others greatly excited.

Scud Sawyer had come to work that morning more belligerent than usual after partying late the night before.

"He acted like he was still drunk," Rosalía said. "He set the forklift too high and stabbed it right through a bin of apples. We heard him swear at some of the pickers, then he drove away. Papá just came by and told us. He drove the tractor into a ditch and tipped it over."

"Oh no! Then what happened?" Megan asked.

"Peter's father fired him. He asked papá to take over Sawyer's work for now."

"Well, something good came out of it then," Peter said.

Nobody was sorry to see Scud Sawyer leave. In the orchard, the other pickers sang and joked. The young man Peter had questioned Saturday stopped by his tree and looked up. "Find perro?" he asked. Peter shook his head.

Aunt Gladys came to the orchard half an hour before quitting time. "I'm going to the hospital soon. Would you like me to run you by the animal shelter to see if there's any news about Jiggs? Then I'll drop you at school."

"Oh, that would be great. Thanks, Aunt Gladys." Peter emptied his picking sack, and he and Megan followed her out of the orchard.

"We'll see you at school," Rosalía called after them.

At the animal shelter the door was locked, but when Megan and Peter walked around behind the building, they saw the attendant feeding the dogs in the outdoor runs. "Hello," Peter called through the wire fencing. "I came to see if anyone brought my dog in."

The attendant motioned them to return to the front door where Aunt Gladys waited. Peter jiggled nervously from one foot to the other. The attendant hadn't said Jiggs was there, but he didn't say he wasn't.

Finally the light came on in the office, and the man unlocked the door. "The dogcatcher just brought in a dog," he told them. "Said someone had found him tied to a tree. I haven't seen him yet."

A hubbub of barks, whines, meows, and yowls greeted them as he opened the door to the holding room. "Let's look in that far corner." He led them down an aisle lined with cages.

They heard a familiar bark. Peter rushed toward a big black dog that was flinging himself against the side of a wire enclosure. "Jiggs! It *is* Jiggs!" Peter cried, sinking to his knees and reaching his fingers through the mesh to stroke his dog's matted fur.

The attendant unlocked the cage. Jiggs bounced against Peter and licked his face. Peter threw his arms around him and hid his face in his coat. Jiggs wriggled free to accept Megan's hugs and pats, then returned, panting, to Peter.

The attendant grinned. "He's your dog, all right."

"Do we have to pay a fine or something to get him out of here?" asked Peter.

"No, but donations to help run the shelter are always welcome."

"We're more than pleased to leave a donation," said Aunt Gladys. She handed a $10 bill to the attendant. "You've made one young man very happy. Thank you."

Peter climbed into the back of the van with Jiggs and ran his hands over Jiggs' back and sides. "He feels thin," he said. "He must be starving."

As Megan reached around to scratch Jiggs' ears, she felt something knotted to his collar. She held up the end of a piece of heavy twine. "How did this get here?" Her mind flashed back to Saturday's scene between Scud and Hulk Sawyer. "The Hulk!" she exclaimed, remembering the broken string dangling from the package rack. "He used twine like this to tie his father's lunch to his bike."

The pieces all fit. Peter must have talked about his dog at school, probably when Sam the Hulk was near. Sam had seen them when he rode his bike away from the ranch. And he'd stopped at the foot of the orchard—probably because he'd seen Jiggs there.

Hulk Sawyer had led Jiggs away, then deliberately abandoned him! Whatever sympathy Megan had felt for the boy flew out the window. And Peter's expression showed that right then, with no concern for the Hulk's size or strength, he would have gladly punched him in the nose.

"We'd better get you two to school now," Aunt Gladys said. "Jiggs will be all right in the van while I'm at the hospital. I'll feed him when I get home."

Megan and Peter entered Miss Vivanco's classroom, eager to tell the Salinas twins that they'd found Jiggs.

But neither of them were there even though Rosalía's last words to them had been "We'll see you at school." Megan felt vaguely uneasy about their absence. So many disturbing things had happened lately. She tried to shake off the feeling by telling herself they'd simply missed the bus.

Next morning, a chilly gray dawn crept in under the edge of low clouds. Peter made sure that Jiggs had plenty of food and water and left him safely tied on the porch where Aunt Gladys could watch him. Wind rattled the apple leaves as he and Megan headed down the hill on their way to the lower orchard.

"Let's stop for Luis and Rosalía," Megan said. "I hope nothing's wrong." In spite of Luis' early distrust, she felt as if the twins had become their good friends in the short time they'd been at the ranch.

They turned into the drive leading to the Salinas house. Peter ran ahead to knock. The lights were on, but no one answered. Then Megan reached the porch, and she knocked. Finally the door opened a few inches. Rosalía glared at them, her eyes red, her hair uncombed.

"Why are you here?" she said in a cold voice. "Did you think I would be picking this morning?"

She started to shut the door, but Peter shoved his foot against it.

"Rosalía, wait. What's wrong?"

"Go away. I don't want to talk to you." She pushed the door closed. They heard her crying on the other side.

Peter knocked and called to her, but she didn't answer. Bewildered, they stood shivering in the wind, wondering what to do.

"Maybe someone has died," Peter whispered. "Or one of their parents might be sick."

"I don't think so," Megan answered. "She acted angry, not sad. Angry at us."

"That doesn't make sense. We haven't done anything to make her angry."

"Not on purpose, anyway." Megan hugged herself and bounced on her toes, trying to stay warm. "Peter, we'd better pray hard. I think something is really wrong."

As they walked along the road to the lower orchard, Megan tried to talk to the Lord about Rosalía, but she scarcely knew what to say. When they reached the orchard, Mr. Salinas told them where to pick. There was no trace of a smile on his face. Once that morning, Megan caught a glimpse of Mrs. Salinas emptying a picking sack. Why wasn't she taking care of the younger children? And once she saw Luis, but he refused to meet her eyes. What could have happened?

"Should we try to talk to Rosalía again?" Peter asked at lunchtime.

Megan considered. "Something awful must be wrong to make her act like she did. I'm kind of scared ... but we're her friends. Let's quit early and see what we can find out."

They saw Teodoro and his baby brother, Juan, playing in the yard as they neared the house. Teodoro saw them and scampered to meet them with a happy shout. Rosalía darted from the porch and scooped up the baby. "Teodoro, come into the house," she commanded.

Grabbing Peter's hand, Teodoro turned. "Why, Rosalía? I want to see Peter."

"Come now. This minute!"

Peter stooped to pick up the little boy and carried him as he and Megan walked toward Rosalía and the baby. Her face was puffy. The anger in her voice had frightened baby Juan, who began to whimper.

She whirled to go back to the house, but Megan stepped in front of her. "Please, Rosalía, tell us what's wrong."

"What is wrong?" Rosalía shouted. Her face crumpled. "You know what is wrong!" Tears ran down her cheeks.

Gently, Megan took baby Juan from her arms and set him down where the boys had been playing with toy trucks.

Peter gave Teodoro a hug as he put him down. "Show Juan how to build a road in the dirt," he told the little boy.

Megan led Rosalía to the steps and sat down beside her. "No, we don't know what is wrong. But we want to help."

Rosalía took a ragged breath. "You can't help. It's all your fault." The tears fell faster. "It's my fault too! All your talk about loving God and praying! I shouldn't have trusted you."

The ache in Megan's chest echoed Rosalía's distress. "But what did we do?"

"You told somebody about papá. Now we must all go back to Mexico."

"No!" Megan gazed at her, shocked. "I didn't tell a soul."

"I didn't either," said Peter.

Rosalía looked up, wanting to believe them. "Then who did?" she asked, her chin quivering. "You are the only ones I ever told."

Megan thought back to that evening in the school courtyard, when Rosalía had told them about her father's arrest and how he had not applied for permanent residency for fear of someone discovering his police record. No one had been close enough to hear ... no one but ... "The Hulk!" she gasped.

"It could have been," Peter agreed. "Remember, when the bell rang, he came from behind the big tree? We thought he couldn't have heard us over all the noise, but maybe he'd sneaked closer than we realized."

Rosalía stared at them. "I remember," she said slowly. She dropped her face in her hands for a long moment, then looked up. "I am so ashamed. Can you ever forgive me? It was not you at all."

"Oh, Rosalía!" Megan gave her a big hug.

"Don't worry about it," Peter said. "But what happened? Why didn't you and Luis come to school last night?"

Rosalía took a deep breath and began the story. The day before, two officers from the Immigration and Naturalization Service had knocked at their door. They'd asked to see her father's green card, the document that proved his right to work and live in the United States. They'd looked at it and at his other papers.

"They could tell that some of them were fake," Rosalía said. "Then they said he was an illegal alien and would be deported from this country in three days."

She wiped her eyes. "All of us. We have three days. Then we go back to a poor little village where Luis and I and the others will be disliked because we are different. Back where I can never be a teacher and Luis can never own an orchard."

Megan stared at her, hardly able to understand what this meant.

"I was so upset, mamá took my place in the orchard today," she said. "I will go pick when the girls get home from school to watch the little ones. We must earn as much as we can to take with us."

Peter found his voice. "No," he said. "This can't happen."

"There is nothing anyone can do, Peter. The law says we have to go."

"There's got to be a way," Megan said. "Maybe the Wirths or Peter's dad can think of something ..." She broke off. "Rosalía, would you let us pray with you? This is a problem too big for us to handle by ourselves."

"Yes, please pray." The other girl's voice broke.

They bowed their heads. "Heavenly Father," Megan began, "You know about this whole awful situation. We don't know what to do, but we know You love the Salinas family and want what is best for them. So we ask You, if it's Your will for them to stay here, to work things out so they can. We pray in Jesus' name. Amen."

Rosalía stood up. She threw her arms around Megan, then around Peter. "I feel better," she said. "Even if we must leave, I will know our friends didn't betray us!"

~~~~~~~~~~~~~~~~~~~~

"But Sam Sawyer did," Megan told those gathered around the dinner table that evening. "I'm sure of it."

"Sam wanted into his father's good graces," Darren said. "And Scud Sawyer wanted revenge. He's made it plain that he hates Mexicans. Carlos Salinas got the job he originally wanted, then took over the job he lost as well. What better revenge than to turn him in to the Immigration and Naturalization Service?"

Aunt Gladys had turned very pale. "Martin's to come home tomorrow," she said. "This is dreadful news, not only for the Salinas family, but for Martin and me. The law provides heavy fines for any grower employing illegal workers. With Martin's injury, the new truck engine, and all the other expenses we've had lately, we could lose our ranch."

Lose the ranch? The thought was overwhelming. "Oh, Aunt Gladys," Megan cried. "What are we going to do?"

═══Unraveling the Tangle

What are we going to do?" Their great-aunt pushed her glasses into place and straightened her shoulders. She gave herself a no-nonsense shake. "We'll do just what Martin and I have always done whenever there's a problem."

She pushed back her empty plate. "Let's tell the Lord all about it right now. Then we will trust Him to show us what to do."

As Aunt Gladys prayed, Megan felt the tightness in her chest ebb away. And when they all said *amen*, she felt sure once again that God would work out everything for good.

Darren Lewis was first to speak. "I can't believe officials would hold you and Martin responsible for hiring an illegal when you believed he was a legal resident," he said. "I'd like to see what the law actually says."

"You know, I think there's something about that law in the information I got from the library!" Megan ran down the hall to get her notebook from her bookbag and brought it back to the kitchen. While Aunt Gladys carried the dishes to the sink, she leafed through the photocopied pages. She pulled out some that were headed *Immigration Reform Act of 1986*.

"I haven't really read these yet." She handed the pages to her stepfather.

Darren studied the document. After a while he looked up, a big grin on his face. "There's a lot of legal language here. But this section seems to say it's unlawful for an employer *knowingly* to hire an alien not authorized to work in the United States. Uncle Martin did not know Carlos Salinas was here illegally!"

Aunt Gladys raised her eyes to the ceiling and said, "Thank You, Jesus!"

Megan rejoiced with Aunt Gladys that Uncle Martin wouldn't be in trouble, but a question still nagged at her mind. *What about the Salinas family?*

Rosalía was back in the orchard the next morning. The four friends picked together but a cold drizzle dampened their spirits as well as their bodies. That afternoon when it was time for school, Rosalía and Luis said they needed to keep picking for as long as the daylight lasted.

Megan and Peter caught the bus alone. The Hulk's suspension was up and he was back in class, subdued. But as Miss Vivanco noted Luis and Rosalía's empty seats on her attendance slip, Sam directed an unpleasant smirk at Peter, then at Megan.

Later in the period, when the teacher gave the class time to work on their reports, Sam found another corner of the room to sit in. Tomás and Eduardo dragged their chairs to Peter's desk. The menacing expressions on their face made Megan feel protective, so she also pulled her chair across to his desk. The two boys sat down and opened their books. Tomás leaned toward Peter and narrowed his eyes to slits. "We hear Luis and his family are being deported," he growled. "What do you know about it?"

Megan gulped. Did they think Peter was responsible?

"Not much," he said. "Somebody told the Immigration people that Mr. Salinas is an illegal worker, so INS said they have to go back to Mexico."

"He can't be illegal," Tomás said. "They have been here for years."

"Rosalía says he didn't apply for amnesty when he should have. Now it's too late."

"Who told INS?" Eduardo questioned.

To Megan, the smirk on Sam Sawyer's face had seemed proof enough of guilt, but Peter hesitated. "I can't say for sure," he said. "But if you want to hang around in the courtyard at break time, maybe I can find out."

"Somebody better do something, or ..." Eduardo made a quick draw-a-knife-across-the-throat gesture. Then he and Tomás casually picked up their chairs and sauntered back to their own desks.

Megan pulled out some papers and pretended to study them. "What did you mean, you can find out, Peter?" she whispered.

"I'm going to try to wring a confession out of the Hulk."

Her eyes flew wide. "No, Peter. He'll beat you to a pulp! And if he doesn't, those other two will."

"Maybe," Peter said. "But I'm fed up with that bully. I want to hear why he stole Jiggs and I want him to admit that he snitched on the Salinas family."

At break time, her throat tight with worry, Megan followed Peter into the courtyard. With the paving still damp from the day's drizzle, not many students lounged there this evening. But she saw Tomás and Eduardo waiting on the bench by the cottonwood.

And Sam the Hulk slouched by the chainlink fence across the courtyard. He stared through the fence and kicked at a clump of grass. Oblivious to the possible consequences, Peter started toward him.

"Peter, you're crazy," Megan hissed.

Peter didn't answer. Megan tagged along several steps behind. The Hulk heard them coming and half turned. His mouth dropped open, then twisted into a sneer.

Peter marched to within a few steps of the Hulk, then stopped and planted his feet solidly. "I want to talk to you, Sam," he began. "First off, why did you steal my dog?"

"Oh, did you lose your doggie?" Sam simpered in mock sympathy. His expression changed to a scowl as he stepped closer and thrust out his chin. "I don't have your dog."

"I got him back," said Peter, standing his ground. "But you stole him. Even worse, you sneaked around eavesdropping and tried to get Luis and Rosalía deported. Admit it."

The Hulk's little eyes flicked up to look over Peter's shoulder, then back to stare at him. "You can't prove nothin', nerd. Get away from me."

Megan quailed at the meanness in the larger boy's face, but Peter kept his voice steady. "I'm not leaving until you tell me why you did it."

"Get out of my way, I said."

The Hulk lunged toward Peter, one massive arm extended to shove him aside.

Peter's control snapped. He flung himself to meet the Hulk. One foot hooked Sam's left ankle while he grabbed the out-thrust right arm. As the Hulk toppled, Peter leaped astride his back, twisting the arm behind him.

The big boy thrashed and squirmed, trying to throw Peter off. Megan screamed and flung herself across the Hulk's legs.

Peter leaned on the arm. The Hulk gave a final lurch and stopped struggling. Peter threw a quick look over his shoulder. He saw Megan. He also saw Tomás standing to one side, Eduardo to the other.

"Man, you got two seconds to talk," Tomás told Sam Sawyer.

From his prone position, the Hulk looked first at Tomás, then at Eduardo. "All right ... all right ... I did take a dog from the orchard. But I didn't know for sure he was yours."

"Then why did you take him?" Peter increased the pressure on the Hulk's arm.

"Oow! I don't know ... I wanted a dog of my own."

"A dog of your own? C'mon, Sam ... then why did you tie him to a tree?"

"My dad said to get rid of him, that's why. Let me up!"

Eduardo moved closer. "Who did you tell about Mr. Salinas?"

The Hulk whimpered. "I didn't ..."

Tomás stepped to within an inch of the Hulk's nose.

The Hulk flinched. "I might have mentioned it to my dad. That's all, I swear."

Peter let go of the Hulk's arm and climbed off his back, giving Megan a hand up as he did so.

"I feel sorry for you, Sam," he said as the bulky youth hauled himself to his feet and backed away.

The bell rang. Tomás, Eduardo, Peter, and Megan headed for the school building, leaving the Hulk alone by the fence.

"Hey, man! Good work!" Eduardo slapped Peter on the back.

A wide smile lit Tomás' dark face. "You too," he told Megan.

Peter looked happy enough to be walking on clouds. He'd taken on the bully—with a little help—and come out the winner over both the Hulk and his fear. "Thanks, you guys. Now we know for sure what happened."

"We know who turned Mr. Salinas in but not what to do about it," Megan told Peter as they filed into math class. A substitute teacher went over yesterday's assignment, explained the new assignment, then told the class to use the rest of the period as a study hall.

Megan finished her math quickly, then pulled out the magazine articles she'd photocopied at the library. One article told how difficult it was for migrant workers to find decent, affordable housing. On some farms,

Megan had seen rows of migrants' cabins crowded close together. She'd hate to have to live like that.

She underlined the facts she could use in her report and picked up another article. This is the one we looked at last night, she told herself, skimming over the pages. Her eyes stopped at a paragraph headed *Legalized Alien Status*.

> The amnesty act provides that an applicant may be allowed one felony charge against his record, or three misdemeanors, unless the offense is a crime of moral depravity.

Was shoplifting a felony or a misdemeanor? She didn't know. Whichever it was, Mr. Salinas could have applied for legalized status despite the offense. None of this needed to happen! Surely shoplifting would not be considered a crime of moral depravity, especially if done to feed a hungry family.

She read on down the page. Much of the material was hard to understand. She stopped and went back to reread a paragraph headed *Family Unity Rules*.

> If one partner filed for legalized alien status before the amnesty ended, the rest of the family may file for permanent resident status.

"If one partner ..." She thought back to the conversation the Hulk had overheard. Didn't Rosalía say her mother had filed to become a legal resident? According to this statement, that made Magdalena Salinas a legal resident of the United States. Therefore, her husband and children should be eligible for legal residency!

Perhaps this was God's answer to their prayers for the Salinas family. Hardly able to contain her excitement, she explained to Peter what she'd read. Then they both watched the classroom clock and willed the hands to turn faster.

When the school bus let them off at their stop, Peter and Megan raced all the way to the Salinas house. But the place was dark.

"Oh no!" Megan's heart dropped. "They've left already."

"They've probably just gone to bed early," Peter said. "Come on, let's tell Dad and Aunt Gladys."

When they walked into the lighted ranch house yard, Jiggs bounded toward them. Peter caught him in his arms and got his face washed with a long red tongue. "I think he missed me as much as I missed him," Peter said.

Megan patted the dog. "I know he did."

The fragrance of freshly baked brownies greeted them as they entered the kitchen. "Uncle Martin's home, right?" Peter asked.

"Yes," said his aunt. "And we've been celebrating!"

"Where are my favorite apple pickers?" Uncle Martin called from the bedroom down the hall.

"Coming!" called Megan. Peter followed her. Martin Wirth lay in the bed, propped up on pillows, and Darren sat in a chair next to the bed, visiting with his uncle.

"Hi, Uncle Martin," said Peter, taking his hand as Megan gave the older man a careful hug. "We're glad to have you back."

"I'm glad to be back. Don't need those nurses fussing over me." He grinned at them. "Besides, I had to come home so I could get a good night's sleep."

"How does your back feel?" Peter asked.

"Better every day."

"The doctor said he'll have to take it easy for a long time yet," his wife informed them from the doorway. "We'll let you get some sleep now, dear."

They all said good night and left the room.

"Aunt Gladys," Megan whispered, as she walked down the hall beside her. "Peter and I need to talk to you and Darren."

Aunt Gladys put her arm around Megan's waist. "This sounds mysterious. How about some goodies first?" In the kitchen, she poured glasses of milk and set a plate of brownies on the table.

They'd not had a snack at break time, and the chocolatey aroma set Megan's mouth to watering. But before joining the others at the table, she pulled the photocopied magazine article from her notebook. As she sat, she pointed out the statements about legal residency. Darren read the section aloud while Megan helped herself to the brownies.

A look of relief and joy spread across Aunt Gladys' face as she listened. "Oh, this is wonderful!" she said. "If Carlos can apply for resident status, as this seems to say, his problem, as well as ours, is solved!"

Next morning, a light rap on the door woke Megan. At her sleepy "come in," Peter stuck his head into the room. "Dad's going to town to check on the installation of the new truck engine. He says he'll take us out for breakfast so Aunt Gladys and Uncle Martin can sleep. Hurry! Get up."

Megan fumbled into her work clothes and splashed cold water on her face. By the time she slipped out of the house to join Darren, Peter, and Jiggs in the minivan, she was wide awake.

They ate at a 24-hour restaurant on the outskirts of Yakima. By the time they finished, the sun was up and shining brightly. Driving into the city, they parked outside a mechanic's shop where a sign advertised "Engine Installations and Repair." The shop's big doors were open, with vehicles in various stages of disassembly crowding the inside. Megan glimpsed Uncle Martin's pickup high in the air on a rack. A couple of mechanics were doing mysterious things underneath.

"I'll see how much work is left," Darren said. "There's sort of a park a couple of blocks up. You guys want to take Jiggs for a walk while I'm busy here?"

"Sure," Peter answered. "Come on, Megan." He snapped the leash to Jiggs' collar. They started briskly down the sidewalk, past other repair shops and places that sold farm machinery. Just beyond a fenced-in junkyard they came to the "park"—a dusty open area with a few cottonwoods and a bench or two against which the wind had lodged foam cups and old newspapers. No one else was at the park, so Peter let Jiggs run free.

After a few minutes, Megan fretted, "The other pickers will be working by now."

They wandered after Jiggs as he nosed along the rickety junkyard fence, then disappeared through a gap in the slats. When Jiggs didn't immediately respond to Peter's whistle, Peter squeezed through the gap to see where the dog had gone. Megan looked around. A few vehicles passed on the street, but nobody else was in sight. She squeezed through after Peter.

A huge jumble of ancient farm machinery and wrecked cars filled the enclosed space. Weeds grew around and through the dead vehicles. Peter caught up with Jiggs at a rusted-out tractor and snapped his leash to his collar. Jiggs strained against the leash, trying to follow a scent.

They rounded the tractor and heard the rumble of men's voices nearby—angry voices, Megan thought. "Let's get out of here before someone sees us," she whispered urgently.

But Jiggs was determined and dragged Peter another couple of yards along the scent trail before his master convinced him to stop. The voices came closer.

"That sounds like Scud Sawyer!" Megan whispered.

"Quick, hide." Peter pulled Jiggs and Megan with him back between the ancient tractor and a wrecked pickup. They squeezed into the space between the tractor's front and back wheels, and Peter clasped his hand around Jiggs' muzzle. Through the weeds, Megan caught the movement of three people.

"We took a lot of risks for you," one of them said. "We want the rest of our money now."

"You'll get it ... just as soon as you do this one last job."

"Burning down a house full of old people and kids— that's more than we bargained for," the third man said. "Besides, you got fired. Where you gonna get the money to pay us?"

Megan craned her neck for a quick look over the weeds, then ducked. "It *is* Scud," she mouthed to Peter. "And the two guys we saw in the orchard!"

Peter's face went pale. "We've got to get out of here."

Scud Sawyer's trademark curse words polluted the air. She and Peter took advantage of the noise to slip around behind the tractor, and as the men's voices moved further away, they crept back to the fence and through the gap. Peter kept his hand over Jiggs' muzzle until they were in the clear. Then they pounded back to the repair shop where they found Darren in the office.

"Quick, Dad, call the police. Scud Sawyer and the guys who sabotaged the reservoir are back there in the junkyard. We saw them—they're planning to burn down Uncle Martin's house!"

Darren took one look at the scared faces of the two young people and turned to a telephone. He dialed 911. He gave the location of the junkyard and told the operator there were intruders in the yard.

In a few minutes, several police cars flashed past the office windows. By the time Megan, Peter, and Darren, plus the mechanics from the shop and others along the street had assembled near the junkyard, the police were escorting three hand-cuffed men out. As one policeman put his hand on Scud Sawyer's head to guide him into the screened-off backseat of the patrol car, Scud caught sight of Megan and Peter. His face flushed dark red. The policeman slammed the door on his string of expletives.

One of the officers came over to the group. "Who called 911?"

Darren stepped forward. "I did. But this is more than a simple case of breaking and entering."

The policeman looked interested. "Okay. What have you got to tell me?" He led Darren, Megan, and Peter over to his patrol car and asked some questions. Megan and Peter told him how they happened to be in the junk-yard and Darren told about the trouble at the ranch.

"All right," said the policeman. "For now, we'll book them for breaking and entering. That will keep them locked up until the owner of this business decides whether to press charges. Meanwhile, you can decide whether to press charges of your own."

"We'll press them," Darren said.

At the police station Darren filled out some papers. On the way home, he told Megan and Peter, "The truck should be finished by tomorrow. The sugar in the gas tank really did a job on that engine. It reacted chemi-cally with the oil and gas to make a sludge that froze up the working parts. They have to replace the fuel line too."

"Is there any way we can prove those guys did it?" Peter asked.

"No, not unless they confess. But the police did get fingerprints off that magnifying lens you found. If they match up, we have a case for arson."

"What I want to know is why," Megan said. "Those drifters were working for Scud, but why did Scud do it?"

Darren swerved to miss a ground squirrel scurrying across the road. "I don't know. I thought all this trouble might be traced back to the company that wants the ranch. But why would it endanger its own reputation and business by hiring people like that? No, there's got to be another explanation."

Citizens of the Kingdom

Back at the ranch, while Uncle Martin napped, Megan, Peter, and Darren filled Aunt Gladys in on the morning's adventures. Then they talked some more about the legal situation of the Salinas family.

"I think we ought to tell Mr. Salinas right now that he might be able to get legal residency," Megan urged.

"We should check first to be sure we're correct before getting their hopes up," Darren answered.

"I'll call the Immigration and Naturalization Service," Aunt Gladys offered, "and see what I can find out."

She looked up the number and, after explaining her errand to several officials in turn, finally reached the head of the local INS. Again she told the Salinas family's story.

When she hung up, she reported, "He says that he'll need to talk to Carlos, but if Magdalena is a legal resident, then Carlos and the children ought to be eligible as well!"

Peter leaped to his feet, muffling a whoop of joy. Megan clapped her hands. "Now we can tell them! Let's go."

In the lower orchard, they found Magdalena Salinas picking with Luis and Rosalía, while the younger girls played beneath the trees with Teodoro and Juan. When a glum Carlos Salinas drove by on the tractor, Darren signaled him to stop. Though Carlos lifted his hand in greeting, Megan thought she'd never seen a man look more dejected. Darren beckoned him over to join his family.

"Listen, everyone," Darren told them. "We've got great news for you!"

The younger children watched, round-eyed, while Darren explained. Rosalía translated his information for her mother, laughing and crying at the same time.

"¡Gracias a Dios!" Tears rolled down Magdalena's cheeks as she pulled Peter and Megan close in a big hug. Her husband's shoulders straightened. The defeated look on his face changed to one of wonder and hope.

Luis turned his head away and wiped at his eyes, then he looked at Megan and Peter. A warm smile lit his brown face. "¡Gracias, amiga, amigo!" he said.

"INS man say we leave tomorrow," Carlos told Darren Lewis. "I tell him we not leave, now?"

"Yes," Peter's father answered. "I'll do your work with the tractor, but first I'll take you back to the ranch house. If Alicia and Isabel can stay with Uncle Martin, Aunt Gladys will drive you and Magdalena to town and she'll go with you to the INS office. Be sure to take Magdalena's residency papers along."

Peter and Megan took their picking sacks from the minivan and followed the twins back to where they'd been working. Carlos and Magdalena and the four younger children left with Darren.

Rosalía's happiness gave wings to her feet. She danced backward ahead of the others, her long braids bouncing on her shoulders. "We can never thank you enough," she sang with a lilt in her voice. "Now we will be real Americans!"

Before they began picking, Megan told the twins about that morning's strange events, and then about Peter's confrontation with the Hulk the day before.

"You really knocked the Hulk down and sat on him?" Rosalía's eyes grew big.

"I didn't *hit* him," said Peter. "I guess I ... tripped him."

"But you sat on him," Megan said.

"Yes. But so did you. He'd have bucked me off if you hadn't landed on his legs."

Luis gave her an amused and admiring glance. "You got into the fight too?" She felt her cheeks turn pink.

"She did," Peter said. "And when Sam saw Tomás and Eduardo standing there, he decided he'd better confess! He admitted that he took Jiggs. And he did eavesdrop, Rosalía, when you told us about your father's illegal status. He said he told his father but no one else."

"Then it must have been Scud Sawyer who turned us in," Rosalía said. "But why? What did we ever do to him?"

"What did Uncle Martin ever do to him, except give him a job?" Megan said. "That's what we can't figure out. Why should he want to cause trouble for anybody?"

"Tomás and Eduardo," mused Luis. "When you first came to school, they did not want me to be friendly with you. They said latino kids had to stick together."

"Is that why you seemed so suspicious of us at first?" asked Megan.

151

"Partly, I guess. I know better now, but I didn't think we had anything in common." He looked embarrassed. "I was jealous of you too because you seemed to have so much. I didn't believe you would want to be friends with us."

"Why shouldn't we be friends with you? Because you're Mexican?" Peter asked. "God made us all different. He wants us to love one another like He loves us."

"What about the Hulk?" Luis teased with a mischievous grin.

"To be honest," said Peter, smiling back, "the things Sam Sawyer does are impossible to love. But I'm asking God to help me love Sam himself. You see, the Holy Spirit worked faith in me. He lives in me, and I know that Jesus died to save me from my sins. Jesus is helping me learn to love other people, even the ones who aren't very likable."

"Even Scud Sawyer?"

Peter laughed. "Yes, but that might take a while."

"God says He loves us all, even people like Scud," Megan told Luis. "But that doesn't mean we should let them get away with hurting others."

They went to work then. Megan and Peter had nearly half-filled their bin before the minivan dropped Darren off at the orchard. He drove by on the tractor and paused where the four friends were picking. "Isabel and Alicia are at the house entertaining Uncle Martin," he said. "But we had to explain all the things that have been going on since he went to the hospital. It was quite a shock to him, and we wanted to be sure he'd be all right before Aunt Gladys left him. While we were talking, a call came from the Yakima police. The two drifters have turned state's evidence, but Scud Sawyer is denying responsibility for anything. They want me to bring you four in so we can tell them what we know."

"When?" asked Megan.

"As soon as Carlos gets back."

Two hours later, Aunt Gladys dropped Carlos off at the orchard. Carlos hurried over to the pickers and pumped Megan's hand and Peter's, his face beaming. "¡Gracias, gracias! All is good ... okay! Papers signed ... we all are legal residents now." He hugged his son and daughter. "Pretty soon, citizens!"

"We can take citizenship classes together." Rosalía beamed at him. "Luis and I can help you and mamacita, papá."

Darren pulled the tractor to a stop and climbed down. One look at Carlos' happy face told him the story. "Congratulations!" he said, shaking his hand. He told Carlos about the request from the police. "Can you handle everything here until we get back?"

"You not worry. All okay!" Carlos took Darren's place on the tractor.

Darren and the four kids piled into the minivan where Aunt Gladys waited with a smiling Magdalena and the little boys. Rosalía and Luis hopped out at their house to clean up for the trip to town. Rosalía translated as Magdalena thanked Aunt Gladys, and added, "She says please tell Isabel and Alicia to come right home."

At the police station, the officer they'd talked to that morning ushered them into a side room where he introduced them to a stocky young man. "This is Detective Alejandro. He'll be handling this case," the officer said. He shuffled through some papers, handed them to the detective, and motioned them all to seats.

Detective Alejandro spread the papers out on the table before him. The little mustache brushing his upper lip curled up on one side, then the other. "Hmm," he said. "This says that the fingerprints on a magnifying glass you brought in match those of one of the suspects. By the way, we have identified two of them as vagrants and petty criminals—last known address was in California." He placed both hands on the table and leaned back in his chair. "You say there have been a number of incidents involving these men. Why don't you start at the beginning and tell me what's been going on."

"It began a couple of weeks ago," Darren explained. "Someone broke down a dike at the irrigation pond and destroyed the pumps. Later that day, a wildfire nearly reached the orchard. The next day the kids found the magnifying lenses you have and figured out how they were used to start the fire."

"Don't forget, someone drained the irrigation pond last spring too," Megan said. "Remember? Uncle Martin said he'd seen two men in the orchard that night. And their descriptions matched those of the men with Scud."

"Yes. I thought at the time that was caused by rodents tunneling, but the men probably did it," her stepfather answered. "We do know for sure that someone put sugar in the ranch pickup's gas tank last week."

He didn't mention the attempt to get the Salinas family deported. Megan knew that was not a criminal act, though it was certainly a sleazy thing to do. And it would be hard to prove that Scud had been intentionally reckless with the tractor in the orchard.

"We heard the two vagrants demand money from Scud Sawyer in the junkyard this morning," Peter said. "Sawyer said no money until they finished the last job. He wanted them to burn down a house. We think it was Uncle Martin's house."

The detective nodded. "Hmm. Yes, the drifters told us about that."

"Why?" Megan asked. "Why would Scud want to do that?"

"I know why."

Five heads turned to stare at Luis.

The detective spoke. "What did you say, son?"

"I know why Scud did it." Luis, who had been staring silently at the floor, raised his head and looked at Megan and Peter. "Remember when you saw him at the packing plant that day last spring when we asked for a ride? He yelled at us about the Mexicans taking all the jobs.

"Later, I was working in your uncle's orchard with my dad when he came to the ranch to ask for work. He had heard that Mr. Wirth needed a foreman, but my dad already had the job. Mr. Wirth asked if he could drive a tractor and hired him to do that. But when Scud saw the foreman was a Mexican, he was really mad."

This was a long speech for Luis. He paused to collect his thoughts, then continued. "Whenever no one else

155

was around, he tried to cause trouble for my dad. Remember the day Mr. Wirth got hurt?"

They nodded.

"I was helping Mr. Wirth fix some apple bins when Scud drove up on the tractor. He saw my dad but not me or Mr. Wirth because we were behind the boxes. He asked my dad to fix something on the front of the tractor. As my dad looked at it, Mr. Wirth stepped out to look too, but Scud didn't see him because he'd turned around and was reaching for something on the tractor."

Megan suddenly knew what Luis was going to say. "I saw him—I saw him bump the gear shift lever into drive," Luis said. "Papá jumped out of the way, but the tractor knocked your uncle down and ran over him. Scud said he didn't know what happened, but I'm sure he really meant to hurt my father."

"So that's why you said Uncle Martin's injury was no accident," Peter said.

"Are you trying to say Sawyer did all these things to get back at your father for taking the job he wanted?" asked the detective.

"I think it started like that," Luis answered. "Then I think he got mad at Mr. Wirth too. He knew about the company that wanted to buy the ranch. Maybe he thought they'd get the blame for what he was doing."

"It's twisted thinking," Darren Lewis said. "But then, from what we've learned of Scud Sawyer and his prejudice, his actions must have made sense to him."

"Well, we've got enough evidence to press criminal charges on the wildfire and the damage to the truck," Detective Alejandro said. "We may not get a confession from Sawyer on the tractor incident—he's probably smart enough not to implicate himself in an attempted murder charge."

"Knowing Uncle Martin, I'm sure he won't want to press charges at all," Darren said. "But I do want you to make it hot enough for those fellows that they'll leave town."

"That can be arranged," the detective said, standing and shaking hands all around. "Thank you all for coming in."

When they left the police station, it was nearly 5:00. "Well, guys, what will it be? School or home?"

"School has already started, and besides, I'm too wound up to sit still for three hours," Megan said. "Let's skip classes this evening."

As they started for home, Megan remembered the film she'd left for developing a few days earlier. They stopped while she hurried into the drugstore to pick up her finished photos. In the minivan, Luis silently studied the shots of people at work in the orchard. Finally, he raised his head. "I'm impressed, Megan. You can almost feel the sun's heat and the weight of the picking sacks in some of these."

"Thank you," she said, remembering his remark that first day in the orchard about her camera being a rich kid's hobby. "I've learned a lot since we came to Yakima Valley. I wanted my pictures to show what a migrant worker's life is like."

"You've done that," he said. "And mamá will love these of Teodoro."

When they stopped to let Luis and Rosalía out, Alicia came running to the van. "Mamacita says can Megan and Peter stay for supper and help us celebrate?"

"That's fine," Darren said. "Aunt Gladys won't be expecting them now anyway."

So once again they found themselves enjoying a party around the Salinas' kitchen table. They passed around the photographs Megan had taken on Teodoro's fifth birthday.

"¡Gracias!" Mrs. Salinas beamed. She taped them to the front of the refrigerator.

Afterward, Luis and Rosalía walked them partway home in the soft darkness of early evening.

"I want to ask you something," Rosalía said. "Earlier today, Peter, you said that you believe Jesus died for your sins and that you believe Jesus helps you love other people. Do you believe that too, Megan?

"Yes," Megan said, surprised at the question.

"I know about Jesus," said Rosalía. "But I didn't know that He cares about how people treat me."

"Of course He does," Peter answered. "Jesus even knows how many hairs you have on your head. He cares about you a lot."

"Does Jesus feel that way about me too?" Luis asked.

Megan and Peter smiled at him and nodded. Then Luis prayed in a halting voice, thanking God for His forgiveness and asking Him for help in forgiving the Sawyers for what they had done. A slow smile spread across his face as he finished.

"God will help you," said Megan, "we're all part of His kingdom!"

Rosalía looked up, her face glowing in the moonlight. "It's true. Because of you, Peter and Megan, we will one day be citizens of the United States," she said. "But even better, we know that we are all citizens of God's kingdom."

"And we're all part of the same family," said Megan. "God's family."

She and Peter said good night to their friends. As they walked on toward the ranch house, she rejoiced in the knowledge that Rosalía and Luis knew Jesus loved them. And she thanked God that He had used her and Peter to help bring an end to the trouble in Yakima Valley.

Glossary

amiga—friend (female).

amigo—friend (male).

beaner—bean picker. Derogatory term for migrant worker.

buenos días—good morning or good day.

buenas tardes—good afternoon.

caramba—an exclamation like "oh my!"

enchiladas—a Mexican dish of tortillas wrapped around
beans, meat, and cheese.

gracias—thank you.

¡Gracias a Dios!—God be thanked.

gringo—derogatory term for white people.

hombre—man, person.

latino—of mixed Indian and Spanish heritage (from Latin).

mamacita—affectionate form of mamá.

mexicanos—people from Mexico.

muchas gracias—many thanks.

niño—little boy.

norteamericano—North American.

perro—dog.

piñata—a hollow papier-mâché animal or other shape filled
with small toys and candies.

señor—sir, mister

sí—yes.

sopapillas—flour tortillas fried then sprinkled with sugar
and cinnamon.

tortilla—flat, thin, round bread made of flour or corn meal.

un momento—one moment.